G. Grove

AT THE RAINBOW'S END

AT THE
RAINBOW'S END

and other stories

DENYS VAL BAKER

WILLIAM KIMBER · LONDON

First published in 1983 by
WILLIAM KIMBER & CO. LIMITED
Godolphin House, 22a Queen Anne's Gate,,
London, Sw1H 9AE

ISBN 0-7183-0229-X

Photoset in North Wales by
Derek Doyle & Associates, Mold, Clwyd
and printed in Great Britain by
Biddles Limited, Guildford.

Contents

I

Pillings For Value

1

It was five o'clock on a bleak October afternoon when I finally made up my mind.

I had been thinking around the subject for a long time ever since I arrived down in the West Country, tramping around in search of work, jingling my few coins in my trouser pocket (the one without a hole). I had considered my position seriously and it seemed pretty grim. I was in my mid-thirties, I had floated around for years, acquiring neither roots nor family, not even possessing a job or a home ...

Sure, there was the dole and social security and all that, but I didn't want any part of them. For nearly twenty years I had at least stood on my own feet, and I didn't want to give up that easily. True, I had known one or two bad let-downs from so-called friends – indeed, just at this rather embarrassing time when I most needed them I didn't seem to have any friends. Still, I'd make out, I'd get by. All day long I had been telling myself that, and jingling my one tenpenny piece and a few twopennies. But then finally the coins had gone, a roll and a cup of tea was all I'd had to eat and that seemed far away and long ago.

So I'd made up my mind, at least I suppose I had. But not consciously, if you see what I mean. It was almost without thinking that I allowed my casual footsteps to turn off the broad pavement and in through the gilt-lined gateways that framed the entrance to Pillings Super Store. I really wasn't thinking about what I was doing – indeed, my mind was on other things. Should I rob a bank? Pull off a post office raid? Swipe some shopper's handbag? Not one of these dramatic actions was really within my compass: I would be far too nervous and scared. But it was nice to imagine.

And so, thus occupied, I drifted into Pillings, along with the hurrying crowds – out of the cold, biting air and into the cosy, warm snug atmosphere inside. Ah, that was better. That was altogether a more pleasant atmosphere. I can remember standing by the escalators, as if on a small plateau among the milling streams ... ladies' perfume to the right, gents' toiletries to the left, hosiery to the south-east, haberdashery north-north-west, jewellery counter far north ... everywhere signs pointing, flashing, indicating, stairs rising and falling, rising and falling, taking with them people, hopes, faiths. I felt suddenly alive and almost important again, caught up in the mesh of this complete and thriving inner world.

PILLINGS FOR YOUR EVERY COMFORT! shouted a great banner hanging on the wall ahead of me.

PILLINGS FOR EXTRA BEST VALUE! screamed another poster.

LET PILLINGS SETTLE YOUR AFFAIRS! cried yet another.

Was it then, perhaps, that I made up my mind?

Maybe. But not yet consciously. Still, as I wandered about, riding on the escalator to one floor, drifting around and then passing on – still I was turning over in my mind wholly abstract matters, ideals beyond realisation. I imagined myself rushing to pick up some wealthy lady's purse, and being handed a handsome reward. I envisaged some complete stranger approaching me, a look of concern on his face, and handing me a five-pound note, to go and buy myself a square meal. Or, drifting, off, I contemplated being left a fortune, unexpectedly, or – or – alas, without even the pennies to jingle, my morale failed to rise very high. Indeed, it sank lower and lower, as I looked around the vast empire, the enormous commonwealth of Pillings Super Store, spread luxurious and abundant before my eyes. What riches! What feasts! What treasures!

It was then – yes, I think about then that my mind turned from totally abstract and therefore quite useless subjects to the pre-eminently sane and immediate one. It was now five-fifteen. Here I was comfortably ensconced in Pillings – warm, centrally heated, extravagantly comfortable Pillings. At five-thirty, bells would ring, doors would close – for me there would remain the inevitable journey out into the cold and bleak, the totally ruthless and cruel world. What would I do then? Where would I go? How would I eat? Where would I sleep? What, indeed, would happen to me, to my physical and spiritual well-being?

Yes, it was then, I suppose, flavouring myself with the sweet scent of warm air inside Pillings, indulging in the comfort of being snugly settled in that hothouse luxury home – yes, indeed, then that I made up my mind.

And so when at five-thirty the attendants went round closing the massive doors – I was nowhere to be seen. I was, in fact, on the third floor, in the furniture and bedding quarters, discreetly tucked away in the bowels of a large Jacobean cupboard. I had finally made up my mind – that a warm and comfortable night's rest in Pillings was very much superior to anything that awaited me in the grim outside world.

I was right, too. But that, as they say, was only the beginning of things.

I waited for nearly an hour until after closing time before I felt it was safe to make a move. I don't know whether you've ever crouched in a cupboard four feet high and maybe eighteen inches wide, for nearly an hour? Try it some time, and you'll feel something like I did when at last, cautiously, I let myself out.

I looked right and left to make sure there was no one about. Then I looked at my watch. Six-thirty precisely. Already it

9

was dark outside. But the lights of all the windows still blazed away, and by their reflection it was easy enough to see my way around in the store.

I had picked the furniture department because I reckoned it would offer the best cover. Also it was on the third floor, well away from the ground. I knew nothing about whatever arrangements big stores made to guard their properties, but I guessed there would be a night-watchman of a sort, somewhere. Maybe, also, policemen now and then looking into doors and flashing their lamps around. But anyway, whatever happened, I reckoned the third floor would be as safe as anywhere. If I kept a sharp ear open, I ought to hear any footsteps in that deathly silence.

To tell you the truth, early as it was, I was already finding things a little on the spooky side. There's something very odd about a place being all hum and activity one moment, and then falling into absolute silence. I mean, there hadn't even been any gradual process: just a few polite goodnights, a bustle of staff disappearing, and then, abruptly – nothingness. Of course, I'd been aware of that silence even in my cupboard: but somehow, now that I'd stepped out, it seemed – well, even louder, that silence.

Still, no use to worry. I considered my position, and I came to a conclusion. I was hungry. Hungry men naturally incline to fix their minds to one purpose – eating.

I looked around. At the end of a carpeted row was a printed list of departments. I crept across, looking around furtively to make sure I wasn't being observed, then began to read the list. Ah, yes, food – the groceries department was in the basement.

I looked around. Too dangerous, of course, to use the lift. I went to the top of the stairs and listened. I couldn't hear anything.

Carefully, trying not to make a noise, I went down the stairs.

It was a long way to the basement. As I approached the entrance to each floor I slowed and waited, listening, my heart beating, especially when I came to the ground floor. But I

10

couldn't hear anything, I couldn't see anyone. And indeed, I reached the basement without incident. Only now I was extremely careful, because I felt sure there must be a night-watchman somewhere, and most probably down here.

However, there was no sign. Everything was still, eerily still: and if anything more spooky than above, for here in the food hall, the floor was as cold as marble, giving a mausoleum effect.

Even as I reached the floor, my nostrils began to quiver. Now I indulged my sensory perceptions to the full. Ah, what luxury! I began to walk around the counters. Naturally the perishable food had been stowed away in refrigerators, but their aroma lingered. And here and there I came across cooked foods that had not been removed. Upon one counter was a whole unopened cheese, only Cheddar, alas, but it seemed as big as a pumpkin. I stood and stared at it in delight, and even caressed its hoary skin with my hands. Then I desisted and moved on, for by now I was increasingly aware of my hunger.

Pillings, I have since learned, are noted for their groceries department. Certainly I had no complaints, on my first evening there as a resident. My only problem was where to begin. On every counter the colourful tins rose in colonnades, outlined by the ghostly light from the street windows. Tins of anchovies, tins of roes, tins of pears, tins of salmon, tins of strawberries, tins of peas, tins of beans – baked beans, plenty of those, bah! – tall tins, bulging tins, narrow tins, flat tins, round tins – everywhere they rose and fell, like waves in an automation sea.

But – my heart sank – of course, I had no tin opener. I looked around hastily. The only sharp instrument I could find was a carving knife from the meat department.

Ah, well, never mind, not everything was in tins. I moved to the biscuits. Here were packets that could be ripped open in a jiffy. I picked out a packet of cheeselets and a box of Swiss cheeses, and took them over to the foot of the stairs, where I could keep cavey with some sort of accuracy. Then, careful not

11

to rustle the paper, I opened them and began eating.

I suppose that is how most orgies develop – a nibble here, a nibble there, gradually building up a cumulative, insatiable desire for more and more? Certainly, in all my time at Pillings I never quite remember a meal like that first one, in which one by one all my inhibitions went. I can remember even now the sensual ecstasy with which I came across a length of salami that had been left out in the cooked meats' section; and then a bottle of cranberry sauce and some pickled onions – with these I made my second course.

Next, I felt like some salad: fortunately Pillings sold very appetising salads already wrapped in polythene wrappers.

By now, though my hunger was appeased, I was all agog for variety, the unknown. I felt pretty aggrieved that I was temporarily cut off from all those delectable tins – especially, now that I felt thirsty, from the tins of fruit. However, thirst was not a difficult matter: further down the counter I came to the soft fruit drinks.

I was about to reach for a bottle of lime juice when my eyes travelled further, and then focussed, rigid with greedy anticipation. There before me, stretching like polished soldiers in immaculate rows, was the produce of Pillings' wine department. Wine, of course, was merely a general name – wines there were, but more, too: bottles of gin, bottles of rum, bottles of brandy. With a sudden movement, feeling rather like the naughty boy in the orchard, I ran across to the wine department, and feasted my eyes on its ghostly contents.

But now, it is rather difficult to remember exactly, but I think that I had almost shed my first cloak of normality. That is to say, when I took the plunge and decided to stay on in Pillings, I gave up my ordinary citizenship – I achieved, by that act, the status of outlaw.

Now, by my indiscriminate eating, followed by my anticipatory onslaught on the drinks, I was willy-nilly committing another decisive step. By staying at Pillings at all, I had committed several crimes, but they were on one level. By stealing food and drink I had reached a new high, or rather

12

low, since this was the ground-floor.

Never mind! I found myself buoyed up by a curious complacency, a devil-may-care attitude that was ideally suited to the circumstances. After all, I had very little to lose. Isn't that rather the way of life? When you have little to lose you are braver, you gamble, you risk all. No? Well, I don't want to pontificate ... I am merely enjoying the pleasure of recapturing the full flavour of that first momentous evening at Pillings.

To the drinks, then. I began with a cocktail – White Lady, I think. Mixing it the correct way, like any expert barman, and pouring it into a ceramic tumbler which the assistant had conveniently left on the counter. Mmmmmmh! That was fine. I'd have another one. And so I did. And then a third ...

Abruptly I sat myself on the counter and looked around, and made a magnificent, slightly tipsy gesture.

'To Pillings – long live Pillings!'

I suppose I must actually have spoken the words. Perhaps I shouted them out. At any rate I was rather startled by the reverberating echo. In my immediate panic, the sound seemed to go on and on, ringing out all over the store.

Clumsily I jumped down and hid behind the counter. I can remember hearing the pounding of my heart. I was not such a brave fellow after all.

But after a while, silence prevailed again. I plucked up courage. Dutch courage, maybe.

Just to sustain it, I had a quick nip of rum. Of all drinks, I have always had a fatal leaning towards rum. I am, as a matter of fact, not much of a drinker at all. But if I want to drink, then it is rum, every time.

That night, it was rum every time for five or six times. That much I can remember. After that things became a little hazy. The floor of Pillings acquired a curious facility of tilting and moving, even of whirling around. I can remember thinking to myself, Pillings is really quite unique, Pillings goes round the customer, the customer doesn't need to go round Pillings. It was, indeed, a solemn thought.

Then, I think it is quite possible I did a little dance across the vacant floor space of Pillings' grocery department. For I have a distinct memory of leaving the wine department and finding myself back among the foods and groceries – green-groceries, in point of fact. Very much among them – for somehow I tripped over and fell full plumb in the middle of the potatoes' counter.

You know how it is, these green-grocers like to amuse themselves by heaping up the potatoes in a vast mountain, each one balanced on top of the other, so that the total effect is pleasing – and one hardly dares to buy a single potato? Well – it was in the middle of this that I landed. Even now I can remember my twin consternations: first, alarm at the noise and fuss it all made, second, terror at the actual effect of the occurrence. I felt myself drowning, yes, literally drowning, under a sea, a cascade, of King Edward potatoes.

In the end, I think it is not too much to surmise, one of the extra large and heavy potatoes must have hit me on the head and knocked me out completely.

At least, that's how I felt when some time later I struggled back into this world. My head was spinning, and I was conscious of pain, and when I put my hand up I felt a sizeable lump on my poor aching head.

'Oh my head! Oh, my poor head!' I groaned.

And then I stopped groaning and stared at the floor in front of me. For there, planted firmly and squarely on that space just in front of me was a pair of man's shoes, and above them the neat crease of a man's trousers – and above that (my eyes travelled up to meet their doom) a man.

2

'Er,' I said.

'Well,' said a voice, deep and resonant. 'And just what are you up to?'

I would have been uncertain how to answer, even if there

had been a satisfactory answer. For though it was bad enough to be discovered, it was especially disconcerting to be discovered not by some beefy but fairly straightforward night-watchman – but by a suave young man in full evening dress.

Yes, there he stood, decked out from top to toe, polished and glistening pumps, neat black socks, tailored trousers, correct double-breasted coat, stuffed shirt and bow tie – just like a sort of tailor's dummy.

Tailor's dummy? I frowned, seeking vaguely for some connection that eluded me.

'I suppose you'd better come with me,' said the young man, with a sigh. 'Come on, up you get.'

I could, of course, have protested or argued. Maybe I could have made a run for it. But hell, what was the use? Where would I run to? As all these thoughts flitted through my mind, I got obediently to my feet. There was, after all, another reason for following the command: I was beginning to feel curious.

Without further ado the man in evening dress led me away down the corridor, between rows of vegetables and fruit, lush pears and Cox's apples, celery and cucumber, lovely round Canary tomatoes – all had rather lost their attraction for the moment.

As I followed him, I studied him by the dim light. He was fair and well-groomed, good-looking in a slightly foppish way. Whatever else he might be, he was obviously not a night watchman; and I doubted if he was a policeman. Perhaps, then, some employee of Pillings, working late? But it was very late, surely: the middle of the night, almost. Would they work quite such long hours?

We came to the lifts, but the young man avoided these, and motioned me to follow him up the stairs that ran from floor to floor on the outside of the swing doors. Once again I was intrigued by his air of complete ease. He must, he simply must have some connection with Pillings, I thought.

At the top floor we went into the household section, great stacks of coloured linoleum, rolls and rolls, curtaining, too, bales and bales of it. The effect created was a curious one of secrecy, of rooms behind walls of linoleum and textiles – their walls rose up to the very ceiling, almost, so that the outside world seemed suddenly faraway, and what lay behind was cosily withdrawn and secret.

We turned a bend, and to my astonishment I suddenly heard the murmur of voices. As we drew nearer, the murmur grew louder and louder ... and louder ... until, with a kind of stupefied amazement, I came to the conclusion it could only be described as a kind of mild revelry.

'A toast to our host!' called out one voice, blithely.

'Hear! Hear!' said another.

'Three cheers for – ' began one.

'Good old Pillings!' said another.

Cheerful voices floated towards me, enveloping me with all kind of astounding details.

'Wait here,' said the young man, and his warning hand brought me to a sudden halt.

I waited there, while he disappeared adroitly between two seemingly impassable rolls of linoleum. A moment later, I detected a sudden hush in the revelry: almost, it seemed to me, an agonised and painful hush: as if in some way the presence of a stranger brought a threat of unimaginable proportions to the carefree gaiety.

I waited, uneasily. Would the curtains part, would I be ushered in upon some fantastic, rabelaisian scene? My imagination boggled at the prospect.

No curtains parted: but after a long pause, from out of the linoleum rolls stepped a new figure, whose only similarity with the younger man was the apparel of evening dress.

Otherwise, I surmised at once, this was a very different kettle of fish. This was a man of about fifty, short, broad, baldish, exuding a curious air of firmness and authority. Where the younger man had seemed vague and almost reed-like, no more, this man conveyed a sense of rugged strength, relentless determination, sheer solidity.

I paused in my analysis, uncomfortable before the piercing

scrutiny of sharp grey-blue eyes. I wished the man would speak, say something, anything, rather than let the silence hang around us with menacing heaviness.

But I fancy it was a good two or three minutes more before relief came, in the form of a series of staccato questions.

What was my name? What was I doing there? Where had I come from? Why had I decided to stay at Pillings? Why not some other store?

This last question seemed so odd that it provoked me at last into speech.

'I've nowhere else to sleep, if you want to know. But anyway, who – ' I gathered my courage. 'Who are you? What are you doing here?' – and as I spoke, I nodded, meaning there, behind the linoleum rolls.

But my inquisitor was not finished yet. More questions, more probings, about my whole life history, but everything put in such a dispassionate way that I could not take umbrage.

At last the questioning seemed near an end. There was just one more, the re-iterated one: What made you pick on this store?

'Well, really,' I said, almost heatedly. 'Does it matter? It was just a store – I was passing by – it looked warm and comfortable, a roof over my head for the night —'

I made a helpless gesture, which seemed in some way to touch the bald-headed man. His eyes softened, and suddenly he reached forward and patted me on the shoulder.

'All right ... don't worry, you are among friends.'

And suddenly, with a hospitality which I had not expected, he stood back and ushered me forward.

'Please enter.'

I stepped between the linoleum rolls.

At once, it seemed, I was transported into a fairy world. Fairy lights there were, indeed, tiny, tiny ones hanging in rows that threw out the faintest of lights – a light that could hardly have extended beyond the thick dark cloak of the walls of linoleum.

17

And by this light, I saw a long table, laden with foods and wines, and laid with beautiful cutlery and crockery – real Wedgwood, I saw at a glance – and tall claret glasses – a table literally groaning under the weight of good things.

And around the table – I had to pause and close my eyes and blink and make sure I wasn't seeing things – around the table sat a company of four, five, six, seven, eight – ten – twelve – twelve people, all in evening dress, sitting down to dinner in Pillings, long after closing time.

But no, it couldn't be?

I looked askance at the bald man by my side. He gave a faint smile. Then he stepped forward.

'Ladies and gentlemen, may I present a new comrade? Mr – er?' He turned and looked at me inquiringly.

'Smith,' I said.

The bald man laughed outright.

'Mr Smith.'

I bowed. And the company, a sea of faces, seemed to turn and rise, and bow back. All of them, old and young, male and female, they bowed politely back to me.

'Sit down.' The bald man pointed to a vacant seat. He looked down the table. 'Will someone pass the wine? A drink for Mr Smith.'

I held up my hand, protestingly. But little notice was taken. I was, it is true, glad to be sitting down. All at once I felt weak, as well as puzzled.

But not too weak to take a curious look at my new companions. Even then, I saw them as a group, as a unity. True, they were a collection of individuals – and yet they were joined together in some subtle way.

I wondered about this, as I looked down the long table. Next to me sat a very strange-looking man indeed, tall and gangling with a huge egg-shaped head and very decisive features – a long, pointed nose and very large, protruding eyes. Next to him was a much younger man, with a mop of curly black hair and keen blue eyes; beside him sat a young girl, hardly out of her teens, a girl with pretty auburn hair and a pair of dancing blue eyes. She was the prettiest sight in the room, I decided: until I looked across the table and saw the woman opposite, a woman of quiet but resolved beauty, a woman more of my own age, with long, smooth dark hair and a lovely, rather pale complexion – ah, now, here was true beauty. I could have feasted my eyes on her endlessly: but there were other faces, an old man with white hair here, and another man of sun-tanned complexion there; an older woman at one end of the table, a stocky man with horn-rimmed glasses nearer to my end and –

'Well, Mr Smith?'

I found that the bald-headed man had seated himself directly opposite me, and was now leaning forward, arms folded on the table – rather like, I fancied, a presiding judge.

'Well ...' I said, with a shrug of bewilderment.

The smile on the bald-headed man's face widened. It was an attractive smile: without it the face might have seemed grim and unyielding, a different face – with the smile, everything about him seemed to lighten and soften.

'My name,' he said abruptly, as if in answer to a question, 'is Ambrose. I won't pretend it's my real name – and I won't pretend it isn't. Who is to say what is real and what isn't? Everyone has a name here, but we never ask whether it is a true one. We only ask that they are true people.'

He paused, and I felt his eyes upon me, keenly. They were deep, rather disturbing eyes, almost black, they seemed to see right through you, into your most secret parts. I could not make out what he was thinking, whether he approved or not of what he saw, whether he was for me or against. I remember, though, feeling a sudden irritation.

'You ask me all kinds of questions,' I said. 'But I want to know what right have you got to ask them?'

I had been about to add, This is a free country, etc. – but I paused in time. What was free about a country that reduced me to this position, and what was free about being here in Pillings, an intruder, a sort of criminal?

As if in some way he read my thoughts, Ambrose went on:

19

'We are all judges, as we are all judged. At some point each one of us has to take responsibility for our actions – some manage to postpone the responsibility, others face up to it sooner.'

He gave a quick gesture towards the assembled company.

'Here, we are all escapists, I suppose you might say. On the other hand, you might equally well say ... ' He paused, and shrugged. 'But perhaps I should leave that to you to find out. What is important, now, is what is to be done about you.'

I looked around, puzzled as they all stared at me. I had no idea what they were doing here, yet they obviously represented some united effort. I felt somehow outside their circle, and rather lonely because of it.

Perhaps sensing my aloneness, the young man who had found me spoke up.

'He seems a good sort, Ambrose. I'm sure he's one of us.' He smiled at me and held out his hand.

'My name's Dick.'

Another man, also quite young, dark and good-looking in a wild, rather romantic way, stood up and leaned across the table.

'And I'll be takin' a chance with you, too. You can call me Liam, and you won't be far wrong with that name. Me father had it before me and his father before him, and sons and fathers hardly ever spoke to one another from the age of fifteen – but still we're tied. I been wanderin' for ten years, and every night I remember my dear father that was ... ' He looked at me with eyes suddenly bright. 'Do you remember your father like that?'

I thought about my own father, dead, like my mother, part of a dim and forgotten past. Perhaps that was what was wrong with me, the cause of my endless restlessness and bitterness, that I could not really remember my father? Was life as simple as that? I looked at Liam, a walking romantic, to whom everything became colour and drama – and I saw that it might well be so.

But all I said, quietly, was:

'I have no father or mother.'

And somehow that seemed to touch a chord among many of those present, as if one of the things they were all united in was a quick sense of pity for the underdog, the defeated, the lost. I saw in their eyes a light of companionship: and dimly I perceived the first of the things that joined them together. A sort of humanity.

'Well?' said Ambrose, looking round the table.

I was conscious of the others studying me silently: then of the white-haired old gentleman raising something to his eyes – yes, it was an old-fashioned pince-nez, of all things. Through it he viewed me steadily.

'This is Mr Grundy,' said Ambrose, a faint note of deference in his voice, as if he were introducing Methusalah, or some other Grand Old Man. Though this old man didn't look to me so much grand or old, as sharp and quick-witted.

'Young man,' said Mr Grundy, in a rather squeaky voice. 'Have you any worldly possessions?'

'Only myself, what I stand in.'

'And what is that, pray?'

I said swiftly.

'Faith ... hope ... charity.'

The old man rather liked that; he nodded his white head like some sage of old. He didn't say anything more, but from the way he nodded, as if resignedly accepting the many ways of the world, I felt he was accepting my presence.

'And Eve,' said Ambrose, 'What do you think, Eve?'

I saw that he was looking at the dark-haired woman. I felt that I wanted very much to know her. Curious that her name should be Eve – she was not altogether like my conception of the original Eve. She looked rather grave and aloof, a woman who had perhaps suffered at some time and now protected herself from people, from other suffering.

I became conscious of Eve looking at me – almost clinically, like a doctor's examination. Annoyed, I met her gaze firmly, almost defiantly. Her eyes were dark and remote – I wondered where she was, herself, her real self.

21

'I think he is honest,' said Eve. And then, with a sudden smile that relieved her apparent hardness, that illuminated her with life and surprising spirit. 'Honest and muddled and ... one of us.'

One of us. Curious how a single phrase can stick in the mind, can come to mean so much. One of us. For days and weeks and months I had been wandering about like a lost soul, wanting to belong somewhere, to somebody, rejected by the world, it seemed. And now, in the most extraordinary circumstances, but unequivocably and without conditions, I was being welcomed as 'one of us'?

It was genuine, too, I knew. I could feel a relaxation in the air, as if suddenly I really had been admitted to the company. One or two of the others spoke; the man in horn-rimmed glasses cross-examined me a little severely, but not really with any malice, the older lady, Miss Starling, said a few kind words – and all at once, I felt at home.

'You see,' said Ambrose, putting one arm around my shoulder in a fatherly fashion. 'We have to be careful, very careful. It's true that anyone who would be wandering around here in the night seeking shelter is pretty well certain to be of our mind, of our circumstances. But one never quite knows. There are dangers all the time, we have so much to lose.'

'Dangers?'

'From the outside world. Here, as you can see, we have created an inside, interior world of our own. It is a secret and very personal world, to preserve it is a task of immense complication. You see, it's like this ...'

Ambrose's voice went on, smooth and precise. I understood everything he was saying, and yet somehow I was not really with him. I was watching the faces around me. It might have been my imagination but somehow each of those faces seemed a little clearer and more defined than before, a little more an individual than a group. I was intrigued now by their differences just as earlier I had been intrigued by their sense of community. I began to wonder about why they had come here. The woman called Eve, the pretty young girl, the

22

romantic dreamer called Liam, the boyish Dick ... the grey-haired man and the white-haired man, the distant and the near, the man with the bulging eyes ...

'I'm sorry,' I said, with a start. 'Forgive me, Ambrose, but I didn't quite hear ...'

Ambrose sat back, smiling patiently. I felt a sudden great warmth towards him, towards them all. I felt as if – as if I was suddenly on the shore, after a long and desperate swim. The shore of an unknown, and indeed very strange land.

'Well, then,' said Ambrose, slowly. 'Listen now, and I will try and tell you the story of Pillings.'

He paused and gave an almost imperceptible and delightful wink.

'Pillings for value ...'

3

I had entered, it appeared, a society within a society. By day, Pillings: *The* Store of the Twentieth Century, was all that it seemed, and employed its many assistants legitimately enough on their tasks of serving customers with their every requirement. From nine o'clock every morning the eighteen swing doors revolved busily as shoppers daily plunged into the labyrinths of stalls and counters and displays in search of everything from ceramic buttons to frozen prawns, from mink coats to vacuum cleaners, from rock and roll records to Steinway grand pianos: the entire mechanism geared up to its maximum effort, hummed like an efficient piece of machinery – even the lifts made their journey from basement to fifth floor in thirty seconds flat, barring the odd interruptions en route from recalcitrant old ladies wishing to reverse direction.

By night, it was a different matter.

'As soon as the last employee has gone,' said Ambrose knowledgeably, 'the night-watchman comes on duty. There should really be more than one for a store of this size, but fortunately for us Pillings consider one lonely inmate enough to guard against the very problematical presence of intruders.

'When I first came to live at Pillings,' Ambrose went on as if he was casually discussing some everyday matter, 'I lived the free and full life of the complete outlaw. One man against one, in a vast enterprise like this – it was child's play. Why, I can tell you some parts of the store are hardly ever visited by the watchman. Since our numbers have increased somewhat, however, we have had to apply more scientific principles in order to preserve our, er, very pleasant way of life.'

Ambrose took my arm and led me away from a corner of the radio department, where we had all been watching a television programme, after dinner. The others remained engrossed. Curtains that conveniently screened off prospective buyers in the daytime just as conveniently screened off any unwonted interruptions by night. Once Ambrose and I had stepped out into the main hallway of the department it would have been difficult for us, let alone a casual prowling watchman, to have imagined what was going on behind that curtain.

Ambrose walked me slowly out of the radio department into the hallway where the lifts operated. He nodded wryly at the closed doors.

'It would be much more convenient if we could use the lifts, but as you'll no doubt appreciate, discretion, in this case is the best part of valour ...'

Smiling, he led me to the stairs and upwards.

'Since you have decided to make your home with us, I thought I had better take you on a brief tour of our, er, territory.'

As Ambrose uttered the last words I shot a quick look to see if some irony or sarcasm was intended: but his face looked quite serious, and I realised he meant what he said.

'You really do look on this as your home, then?'

'But, of course.'

We climbed steadily upwards, until we came to the very top of the stairway, and at a gesture I followed Ambrose out through swinging glass doors on to Pillings' famous roof garden.

' ... what better home could one wish for?'

Ambrose paused, and indicated the gentle, undulating slopes of rockeries and lawns, shrubberies and flower beds, complete with miniature waterfalls and lakes, the whole conveniently illuminated by the permanent lighting. All around us the air was fragrant with the scent of hyacinths and foxgloves, geraniums and polyanthus.

'In the hands of a first class gardener,' remarked Ambrose, catching my eye. 'A man who spent four years at Wye College before taking up an important post at Kew Gardens – oh, to be sure, Pillings always aim at the best quality.'

We began to stroll along the crazy pavement pathways, between neatly cultivated beds of flowers. Once Ambrose bent down and picked a red rose, sniffing at it appreciatively before putting it in his button hole.

'Would you like one?' he enquired, quite naturally. 'There, what about the one over there? White and very pleasant.'

I took his advice and picked the white rose. It smelt divine. I put it in the button-hole of my coat, aware of an added sense of well-being.

'I can see,' I said, 'that Pillings is going to teach me to appreciate the good things of life.'

Ambrose's face creased with laughter. How alive he looked, not half as old as his years – how alive and young we would all look if we laughed much more.

'I'm glad you have a sense of humour ... because one needs a sense of humour even in order to be serious about life. The fact is that living at Pillings will teach you many things my friend. How to appreciate – life itself. At least, I hope so.'

He turned and looked at me intently. I felt in some way that as yet he was not sure of me, and I longed suddenly to reassure him. I also felt impelled to a curious honesty that was not always so forthcoming.

'Look here, I want you to know from the start that I came here – I came here because I was down and out, not because I sought some new way of life, or anything like that. What I mean is, don't expect too much of me, will you? I'm only a –'

' – poor mortal – I know, I know,' said Ambrose, almost impatiently. 'Don't you understand that everyone who came to Pillings came the way you did? They were all tired and dispirited, defeated and downhearted – their wives had left them, or their businesses had gone wrong, or they had suffered in some way or another so that their normal worlds had collapsed. The reasons aren't important – what matters is that they came in despair – and they found something they least expected.'

'What was that?'

Ambrose shrugged. He pulled out a packet of cigarettes, expensive Turkish cigarettes – I remembered a display of them in the wine section – and offered me one. We lit up and puffed appreciatively.

'Hope,' said Ambrose at last.

It was getting chilly, so we left the gardens. As we went down the wide stairs, Ambrose began to explain the general layout of the stores.

'It's grown up in rather a disorganised fashion, has Pillings.' Ambrose spoke almost disapprovingly, like a master about his pupil. 'We feel that the time has come for a big re-roganisation – but Pillings don't seem as yet to feel the same.

'For instance, having the food counter on the ground floor is a most inconvenient arrangement,' he went on, dead-pan face, so that we were on the next floor down before I guessed that this time there was irony.

The fourth floor of Pillings, as Ambrose now demonstrated, escorting me confidently around the maze of stands and displays, was given over to china, pottery, wrought iron, hardware, and other decorative processes. In the darkness, however, it was impossible to study the display with any real interest.

'Nevertheless, please remember,' said Ambrose, in passing, 'this is the floor from which all domestic requirements are to be obtained. You know how it is – one is always breaking something, a cup or a plate, or a soup bowl – they have some most exquisite Wedgwood soup bowls by the way. Not the ones on show, of course, never touch those. But just look behind the counters and you will find plenty of stock.

'You just take them – as you want them?'

'Naturally.'

Ambrose said no more, as we walked back to the stairs. And from the way he walked, the way he held his head, reflectively, obviously lost in other thoughts, I began to appreciate that 'naturally' was just the right sort of word.

Indeed, as we progressed on our tour, visiting the third floor (women's wear, children's), skipping the floor where the television session was still in progress, calling in at the first floor (footwear, fabrics, textiles) – I began to understand why Ambrose spoke with such confidence.

'But you have everything,' I said, with rising excitement. 'Absolutely everything you want, at your finger tips. Why – it's wonderful, marvellous – it's like a miracle.'

We had paused at the men's wear, a department that was partially lit by the evening lights shining through the windows. Here were elegant Savile Row suits, sports coats and trousers, overcoats, raincoats, swimsuits ...

'In the morning,' said Ambrose casually, 'you'd better pick yourself something off the ready-to-wear counter. I noticed your present suit has worn, shall we say, rather threadbare.'

I stopped, gaping.

'In the *early* morning, of course,' said Ambrose with a smile. 'Just after dawn – that's when we pay our visits for individual items like clothes.'

'And I suppose the night-watchman is generally half asleep by then?'

Ambrose didn't seem to hear me, so after we had gone down to the ground floor I repeated my remark. He did not answer, but seemed in some way amused.

'You did say,' I went on, 'that the watchman made his rounds – isn't that always a potential danger?'

After a long time, Ambrose nodded his head.

'I suppose you might say ... Yes, potentially ...'

But obviously the thought of the night watchman did not

27

worry him unduly. Otherwise, I reflected, he would surely have muffled his footsteps more effectively as we came on to the ground floor, the show place of the store, wherein the tremendous night hush I would have thought a pin, let alone a foot, would have echoed and re-echoed in the ears of the anonymous night watchman.

Ambrose beckoned me to the stairs leading to the basement.

'Here, are you sure it's safe to go down there?' I asked, half protestingly.

Ambrose was already halfway down.

'Of course – come on. I want to show you the sports and games department, most amusing.'

'And more reasonable to visit, as it's in the basement,' went on Ambrose. 'It's relatively safe to throw a little light on the subject.'

When we were down he pulled a couple of switches and lit up a corner of the games counters, spotlighting a table-tennis table.

'Do you play?'

I hesitated.

'Well, yes, but … ' I looked round nervously for the night watchman. I supposed Ambrose knew what he was doing.

'Come on then,' he said cheerfully. 'Best of three games.'

We were soon at it hammer and tongs. I hadn't played for some time, and Ambrose was obviously expert from regular games. But after losing the first set I began to get my eye in, and made one or two winning shots that brought appreciative grunts from my opponent.

In fact, it was just after one of these, while Ambrose was bending down to pick up the ball, that I looked casually across the floor and froze with horror at the sight of a man standing and watching us – and watching, I guessed, was the operative words, for the man did not wear evening dress, but the uniform of Pillings, blue and striped, and peaked cap.

Instinctively I turned and ran, racing over the polished floor, leaping the counter containing golf clubs and sending them flying.

I was nearly at the stairs, ready to hare up them and out of Pillings for ever – when Ambrose called after me, almost irritably:

'Whoa back, there's no need for panic.'

At the sound of his voice, unworried, absolutely normal, I halted, so to speak, in mid-air. I hesitated, turned, and rather sheepishly, walked back into the lighted area.

Ambrose was seated by the table, in the act of handing a cigarette to the night-watchman.

'I suppose your jumping to conclusions is natural,' said Ambrose, comfortably. 'But there's really no need.'

He swung round, indicating the other man.

'I want you to meet this member of our community. Sam, this is, er, Mr Smith. He is joining us.'

I stared at the man, a thick-set, burly, Cockney type. He grinned and offered a plump, horny hand.

I made a bewildered gesture.

'But – isn't this the night watchman?'

Ambrose smiled faintly.

'Oh, yes ... Sam's the night watchman all right.'

He puffed at his cigarette.

'One of the many things we have learned from our sojourn at Pillings is – it's better to absorb your enemies than fight them.'

4

I was given a berth in the furnishings department. The term berth was explicitly used by Ambrose when he gave me his instructions: I came to realise that it was accurate enough, Pillings *was* something like a mammoth container or ship. It was an amusing idea to play with, that of a vast liner with its secret cargo of escapists ... but no, at the moment, I had no time for playing at dreams. I had work to do, a place to establish, a berth of my own to create.

It was more difficult than I had imagined: and yet

experience taught me that Ambrose was right in his insistence of each one of us having our own berth, our own private corner of Pillings. True, in many ways our life at Pillings might well be compared to that at a luxury hotel. We had the run of the usual departments, with our own writing room, our own rest room, games room, etc – bathrooms, too, for Pillings were especially attentive to the hygiene of their staff and every floor had large toilets and showers. As with the best hotels, we had a roof garden in which to wander undisturbed. For reading matter, up to date, too, we had only to wander into the book section, with its liberal array of new novels and biographies. There was even an art gallery at our disposal, should we feel culturally minded.

Yet even hotel guests had their own bedrooms to which they could retire, a certain sense of privacy even among so much public exposure. And we, like hotel guests, were human beings, we had the same natural desire for a tiny spot where we could drop our masks and be alone with ourselves – a much more difficult task, really, than being alone with anyone else.

So Ambrose was wise to allocate us our berths, even if the name was rather misleading. What he meant, in effect, was that each one of us was offered a site somewhere in the store where we could make up our own little resting place. We could within reason take our choice of available equipment, with the obvious condition – whatever we used must be back in place an hour before opening time. There were very few rules in our lives, but those that there were applied rigidly. One result was that all of us lost the chance of the favourite English occupation, a lie in bed in the mornings, for the rise by seven rule was sternly enforced, and we even had a rota system of sentries to go round waking everyone up. However, as with everything else in life, one soon adapted oneself to the circumstances, and after a time even savoured the advantages. I shall never forget the many beautiful dawns I watched from the roof garden at Pillings, the new-born sun hovering shyly over the city rooftops.

My first berth, then, was in the furnishings department. I wasn't, it's true, allocated the actual bedding section, since this was given over to the feminine side of the community. Eve, for instance, slept on a beautiful modern divan in one corner, with a lacquered screen around; Ann, the pretty young girl, had a smart modern bed nearby, and the grey-haired woman had made herself at home on one of the popular new bunk beds.

Myself, I chose a secluded corner of the garden furnishings, a place full of wicker chairs and seagrass stools and tables – and, as my sharp eye for comfort had observed, an elaborate and positively luxurious hammock couch affair. You may have seen these in your own local store windows, quite elaborate affairs with brightly coloured canvases and tops and sides. However, I doubt whether you have seen quite such a luxurious hammock couch as the one that now became my nightly resting place at Pillings. It was the most exotic type I have ever seen and it was one of the joys of my life until the black day, a few weeks later, when some wealthy business man bought it for an idle whim.

From the moment I was allocated a berth, I lost much of my initial nervousness. The whole episode of that evening had, after all, been enough to drain anyone of their nervous energy. I had still been trembling from the shock of the encounter with the friendly night-watchman when Ambrose took me up for a final nightcap of whisky.

'You know, for the past three nights I've been sleeping rough,' I told Ambrose, just before saying goodnight. 'I can't seem to forget ...'

'You must,' said Ambrose, simply. 'Here you are beginning a new life.'

I slept like a log. I was so tired, so weary, and on top of that, so well fed and drunk – I don't doubt that I would still have been sleeping like a log at nine o'clock in the morning when the store opened ... In fact I am not sure that I wasn't immersed in a nightmare around that theme – the hammock swinging furiously from side to side in the hands of an enraged shopwalker, the entire staff peeping behind him in horror, maybe Mr Pillings himself approaching like a figure of Doom – when I suddenly started awake.

I *was* being shaken, but by the friendly figure of Liam, his dark Irish hair falling over his face and his bright brown eyes still heavy with sleep.

'Come on, now, me boy, be a-stirring yourself. 'Tis bad enough having to wake meself up without all the heavy labour of shaking the likes of you.'

I looked ruefully at my thin figure.

'I only wish I was fatter.'

Liam smiled.

'Ah, well, not to worry. A month at Pillings' expense and you'll soon put on the pounds. Look at meself, now, all svelte and well fed – when I came here I was just a skeleton, you might say.'

'How did you come here?' I asked, sitting on the hammock and starting to dress.

Liam leaned against the tubular railings. He was always at any time, I discovered, ready to ramble off without any thought of time or people or place. Once, so I was later told, he overstepped himself in this way with Alfred, the popping-eye man whom I had discovered to be a comic poet, and the two of them were still in a corner of the store, arguing when one of the under-managers arrived early. However, Liam being Liam and Alfred being Alfred, they managed to talk themselves out of an awkward situation by saying they had found a door open and were in such a hurry to inspect some goods they had just taken a quick early peep. And they would like to order this, please, and that, please, and probably a lot more ... but they would just like to fetch their wives back to make sure which patterns, etc ...

'How did I come here?' said Liam, looking dreamy. 'Ah, well, now, 'twas a wet day in November and I was busking –'

'Busking? You? I wouldn't have thought that.'

'And why ever not? Sure and I have a fine rich deep voice, as I will now proceed to demonstrate.'

32

Liam took a deep breath; but I hastily quietened him.

'Never mind, I believe you. But how –?'

'Well, and I'd been busking on and off for six months, earning quite a good wage – and before that, do you know, I did furniture removing – there was always something going like that. Meself, I niver had much trouble in finding a job – course, I'm easy and adaptable, and some folk ain't. But then, this day I was tellin' you about, there I was, singing for me supper – and suddenly I just felt fed up with the whole thing. I thought to meself, what the merry hell, whey should I devote the best years of my life to existing in this desultory manner – for that's what it amounted to, I was singing in order merely to exist, exposing meself to the public stare for the sake of a few pounds.'

'So?'

Liam sighed, and then grinned engagingly.

'So – I'm afraid the rest of the story isn't very dramatic. I went and looked for my friend Alfred, who'd been looking exceptionally well-fed and prosperous, and I said, Alfred, me boy, the time has come for me to join you in your new life of leisure. I knew he was on to something, you see, but I didn't know quite what ... And Alfred, he just looked at me very long and considering, like, and I suddenly had the feeling that I was a man whose whole life was being weighed in the balance, and indeed it was – for how awful, if he had decided not to let me in on the little secret and I had none of this knowledge at all of a better world existing – anyway, the good fellow that he is, Alfred just nodded and said, "Meet me for a drink tonight and all your troubles will be over".'

Liam stirred his lanky frame.

'And, begorra, as the Irish are wont to say, so they were. Come on now, bully boy, time to be moving, I've others on me roll call.' He winked. 'Mind you, one or two of them, well, waking them up is a pleasure, a real pleasure. Like little Ann, for instance.'

I finished dressing and stood up.

'Are you fond of Ann – is she your girl, I mean?'

Liam burst into laughter.

'Come now, my friend, do I look a baby snatcher? She's a dear little kid, that's all.'

'Now Eve,' Liam continued, with a touch of reverence in his voice. 'There you have the most wonderful woman who ever had the misfortune to be born out of Ireland. Alas, alack, she won't take me seriously.' He eyes me quizzically. 'Happen she might take someone like you more so?'

I blushed.

'Well, I don't really know her. In fact, perhaps you had better explain the general set-up to me.'

'Tomorrow,' said Liam soothingly. 'There's plenty of time. Tomorrow ...'

Which was, of course, really today. Yes, a new day had dawned all right. It was some time since I had been up so early, but now as I moved about in the dim early light I began to feel curiously excited. Everywhere the sunshine was pouring in through the wide windows thoughtfully installed by Messrs Pillings. And by this bright light all the mundane and quite ordinary things seemed to be imbued with exciting personality.

It was a strange experience, early that first morning in Pillings. Moving about my new kingdom, and constantly being startled as I stumbled across a sleeping body, or an apparition greeted me between the cupboards in the kitchenware department, or someone gave me a start by seeming to materialise from out of the china and pottery displays. By now I was beginning to recognise faces, I was feeling at home.

We all had breakfast around a coffee demonstration stall that was conveniently placed in the food section. As I queued up, I found myself behind the man with the bulging eyes, whose name I had learned was Alfred Blossom. I had also been told he was a poet of no mean talent: but it seemed a little early in the morning to dwell on his cultural attainments.

'Tell me,' I said. 'How many people live here altogether?'

'Ah ... ' Alfred's voice was a booming, echoing one, and for a moment I was embarrassed, thinking they would all turn and stare; but they must have been well used to it, and nobody paid any attention.

'*Quality*, not quantity, is what counts in life, young man. How many poets are there in the world? Perhaps a hundred thousand? Perhaps poets all lined, sitting at their little desks, writing their hideous little poems, which hardly anyone will ever read ... No, the mind boggles. Shall I tell you, *really* how many poets there are in the world?'

Alfred held up the fingers of one hand, and then, rather more dubiously, of the other – but clenching several, to indicate that the total might be seven or eight at the most.

'And *where* are these poets? Undiscovered, most of them, living furtive lives under bushes – like me. I am a poet, young man, in case you didn't know. My poems have appeared in many of the best magazines, and yet, do you know, I am not only a poet, but a penniless poet ... a penniless prejudiced poet ... Aha ... that's rather good ...'

In the end I got my coffee and escaped. I had begun to realise from a strong flavour of whisky that was breathed over me that our poet was even at the hour of seven-thirty in the morning, slightly inebriated.

But when I commented on this to some of the others, they were not critical.

'Don't forget, we all need our escapes,' said Ambrose. 'I don't know yours yet, but Alfred's happens to be the bottle. Don't you think perhaps everyone should be offered their escapes? It makes them in a curious way free – free people. You see, it forces them in the end to face up to themselves – or give up altogether.'

Ambrose was full of remarks like that; but he was also a very human sort of man. I am afraid I may have made him sound something too saintly, a bore, even. Let me correct that impression. From the moment I met him he seemed strangely familiar. I felt at ease with him, at home – yes, at home, that was the right expression. He reminded me vaguely of my own father. It was not that he looked like my father, but there was something of that solidity, that reliability, that readiness to take authority which we connect with our parents.

And yet, he was far from a father figure, don't think I'm suggesting that. Maybe some of us tended to make Ambrose such a figure, for our own ends – but he was not himself so constituted. Above all, he was more like a conscience. He would never if he could avoid it pronounce a definite order or directive – if you asked him to settle a problem he did so by asking you what you felt was best. He threw the ball straight back. He refused to provide an easy way out, he forced you to face the truth if he could.

It was Ambrose who began the whole thing, who discovered the possibilities of Pillings, that child of the apparently eccentric brain of one Orwell Pilling, one of those supposedly wealthy barons of the departmental store world. I knew very little about Orwell Pilling before I went to accept his unbidden hospitality, but gradually over a period he began to assume proportions of a human figure – but always one in the background, a shadowy conception. At least beside the reality of Ambrose. Orwell had created Pillings; but Ambrose, I often felt, had brought it to true flowering ... He seemed so much at ease, so self-assured, that I found it hard, sometimes, to believe that he had not always been there, as permanent as the sculptured figures over the entrance, or the marble hallway and the gilt railings.

I remarked on this, as I helped to wash up the breakfast things, and found myself side by side with Eve. To tell the truth, I found myself absurdly nervous in her presence. She had a coolness, a remoteness, that was almost frightening. That was perhaps why I spoke quickly, almost without thinking, in asking about Ambrose.

For a moment she did not answer. She went on washing the plates, her long, graceful neck bent so that the dark hair fell forward, hiding her from me.

Then, just as I was going to say something else, she spoke.

'If I were you, I would ask fewer questions, until you have been here longer.' She looked at me, her eyes not unfriendly. 'I know it's tempting ... but how do you know you'll get the right answers? When you ask how long Ambrose has been here, would it really matter if I said one year, two years, three years? Surely what matters is that he is here, that we are here, that this world exists?'

She was quite a one for the existing situation, was Eve. She believed implicitly in the moment – in making the most of each moment as if it was your very last. I must admit she was a fine testimony to her own beliefs. She was what by any standards would be called a fine figure of a woman: tall, graceful, with strong shoulders and strong features, and almost jet black hair brushed straight back and down. There was something almost Spanish about her appearance, her way of walking and moving – she seemed so alive, so aware of herself, that I was quite surprised when she told me she was, in fact, Welsh.

'Eve – surely that's not a Welsh name?'

'Didn't you know? Eve was a Welsh girl. Adam knew ...'

I couldn't help laughing. But I laughed as much with relief at discovering that she had a sense of humour as at what she said. I could feel myself being attracted very strongly to this woman: but if she had had no sense of humour I would have fought against it tooth and nail – for there is nothing in the world worse than a humourless woman.

How nice not to have to fight: I flirted mildly with Eve for quite a while until there was suddenly a hushing sound, and everyone quickly finished what they were doing. Taking my cue from the others, I joined a sort of general assembly in one of the entrance halls.

I noticed that while we assembled one or two people rushed round finishing the tidying up. Only when they had completed their tasks and signalled so, did Ambrose speak his little piece.

'Good morning, friends. Well, another night is safely over, and let's be thankful, as always. May I ask if everyone has followed the usual procedures?'

There was a faint and confident murmur, in which I found

myself joining.

'Good,' said Ambrose. He looked at his wrist-watch. 'There remains nothing to be said except please proceed to your usual stations and carry out the normal dispersal at 9 a.m. precisely. I hope you all have a pleasant day out.'

He paused, and then almost as if just remembering.

'Oh, and of course, if anyone needs funds, would they please contact Mr Grundy as usual?'

5

It was some time before I realised that I was very much among those who would be needing funds.

By then I was at my action post, and it was too late. Just as the routine for getting into Pillings and staying there when applied to more than a dozen people was quite complicated, so the routine for getting out of Pillings was also difficult. However, someone, Ambrose no doubt, had worked out a very simple and skilful method. We took up secret positions at selected places all within a radius of about twenty feet from one of the main doorways. As there were some eighteen doors into the store, this was not such a difficult feat as it sounded. We gathered in tiny groups of two or three by several doorways ... I was with Alfred, the poet, and the young man called Dick who had been the first to find me the previous night. Alfred was inside a large contemporary cupboard, and Dick lurked with the skill of long practice between some displays of ladies' underwear. I, being regarded as something of a greenhorn, had been given as easy position, standing directly behind a huge sign which said in bold lettering: WELCOME TO PILLINGS!

At a quarter to nine the night-watchman made his appearance, going round unlocking the front doors. Then at nine precisely, the members of the staff, who had assembled dutifully outside, pushed open the doors and hurried in to take up their posts.

It was during the thirty seconds or so after they had entered, and were busy disappearing to their respective floors that the night inmates quickly sidled out of the door. A foolproof system, really, for the moment we were outside we might easily be taken for passers-by staring in at the windows – indeed, part of the routine was for selected members to take their time and window-gaze before wandering away, thus dispelling any danger of rushing figures catching the eye.

All the same, I was relieved when, at three minutes past nine that morning, I found myself walking down the High Street, a free man again, with Dick one side of me and Alfred the other. At least, one moment Alfred was with us – the next he seemed to sidle away.

'Alfred knows something we don't,' said Dick with a smile. 'A place where he can get a drink at nine in the morning. Myself, I just couldn't face it.'

'And I can't afford it,' I said. 'Or anything else ... I feel rather a fool – I gather that Pillings not only provides us with a home, but cash, too?'

Dick laughed.

'Well, within reason. We have a system of what you might term delicate filching. It's not done on any scale, we are always careful not to harm our benefactors. Ambrose reckons that their annual profit is at least 100 per cent, so a little loss won't do any real damage. It's too complicated to explain to you now how it's done.'

He looked at me quickly, possibly detecting my sudden appearance of dejection.

'But don't worry, I can led you a few pounds to get through the day, and you can pay me back tomorrow.'

Somehow Dick's offer was the last touch needed to make the glorious sunny morning complete. I had just emerged from one of the most extraordinary nights of my life, and it was only the momentary memory of my previous poverty that had thrown a damper on my spirits.

Now, free of that, I felt exhilarated. I began to hum to myself for sheer joy – so joyous was I, in fact, that I began to intrigue Dick, I think, for he kept smiling at me, and finally threw an arm round my shoulders.

'I like you, my friend. You're one of us.'

I clapped Dick on the back.

'You're right. I feel fine. Come on, let's take a walk in the park, and you can tell me all about us.'

We went into the park and walked down to the lake. Little boys were sailing their toy yachts, and several nursemaids were out wheeling prams. I noticed Dick eyeing one or two of them in what might be called a speculative manner. He was a good-looking boy, and I was not surprised when the nursemaids flashed back smiles of their own.

But Dick made no attempt to pursue the invitations. Instead, he picked up a blade of grass and stuck it on one lip and walked along, whistling a cheerful tune.

'Girls,' said Dick, with a quick sideways glance. 'Do they interest you?'

I shrugged. I felt bitter about women. I had been married once, and it had proved a great mistake. Most of my other connections with women had been rather on the same lines. In the end, my self-esteem hurt, I suppose, I had retreated into myself.

'Not much.'

'Mmmmmmh,' said Dick, in the tone of one trying to imagine a world in which girls were not much interesting, and finding it difficult. 'Myself, I like 'em. They seem to me the answer to everything. I never feel unhappy when they are around, I don't mind if it rains or shines, snows or hails – just give me a nice, warm-hearted cuddly girl, and a seat in the park or a corner of a corn field on a sunny day ... Mmmmmmh.'

I couldn't help smiling. There was something almost child-like in Dick's manner. He seemed to me perpetually young and innocent, though he would have been insulted probably if I had told him so.

'Who is your girl then?' I nodded over my shoulder at a hypothetical Pillings. 'I mean, back there.'

'Oh, no one there,' said Dick hastily. 'I mean, I flirt around with young Ann sometimes, just for a lark, you know, but nothing serious. Oh, no, that would never do – never mix home and away so to speak. Plenty of time for girls in the daytime if you want them.'

He looked around appreciatively as a couple of soignée young girls went by. 'I mean, the world is full of them, old boy, isn't it?'

I smiled, thinking – that's easily said. But how to choose, who to choose? In the back of my mind I carried an image of Eve, cool and serene at the washing basin: she affected me strangely.

'What do you mean,' I said abruptly, 'about not mixing – is there a rule or something, about one's personal relationships?'

'Good Lord, no, I don't think so. I just meant for me –'

Dick swung round in sudden confidence, looking at me with his open and innocent eyes. 'You see old boy, I just can't help tending to get mothered a bit, I seem to affect women that way. And then – well, I guess I became a damn nuisance ... It wouldn't do for me to be someone's lapdog, back there. Why, I wouldn't like it myself. You see ... well, that place is like home to me, the first real home I've ever known.'

I looked at Dick quickly; but I could see he was quite serious.

'You see, I was an orphan. Never saw my mother or father. They were killed in a car smash when I was about six months old, and there was no one else at all, so I ended up in an orphanage.' He gave an ambiguous laugh. 'Never spend too long in an orphanage if you can help it, old boy. However, I survived ...'

Survival, in Dick's case had meant the usual round of degradation, running away twice, appearing in a juvenile court, all kinds of petty trials and tribulations which to some extent shaped his life.

'Not that I became a crook or anything like that ... Matter

41

of fact, I went into the car business, buying and selling ... still do it now and then ...'

Dick went on with sudden enthusiasm to elaborate on some of the superior cars he had dealt in, but I hardly listened. I suddenly saw him as the bright, cherubic young car salesman, imagining how effective he would have been – who could resist his ready charm?

'I'm sure you were good at a job like that. What on earth made you come to Pillings?'

Dick looked surprised.

'But, old boy, I've told you. It's the first real home I've had. And that's worth an awful lot, believe you me.'

We went into a cafe and had some tea. The morning spun on. I listened to Dick's rambling talk, and then after a while only half listened. I spent the rest of the day like this, part of the time with Dick, part on my own.

It was strange to be wandering about like a visitor, and to feel secure. That was the most unusual, the really unique sensation of that day. For weeks I had never been quite sure when my next meal was coming, or where from – nor where I would sleep the night. Suddenly I knew that these things were provided, and I felt a different person.

Consequently the day itself was coloured by this understanding: it became one of the gayest, freest, happiest days of my life.

When I arrived back at Pillings, shortly after five o'clock that afternoon, I felt airy with happiness as I mingled with the crowd of shoppers. There was still half an hour to go before closing time, but I had been rehearsed in my instructions very carefully. Mingle with the crowd, then make for the linoleum department. At the far end you will see an opening into the storeroom. While inspecting the linoleum, choose a quiet moment to pass into the store-room, and there secrete yourself behind some bales of Indian carpets. Remain there until further notice ...

Further notice seemed to me to take a very long time, but I suppose it wasn't bad. Six-thirty precisely I was awakened to reality – my new reality, that is – by a whisper from the doorway.

'Well, you can come out and frolic,' said Liam.

I followed Liam out of the store-room and into the basement, lit faintly by central bulbs. In a far corner, where he had his corner office with a small electric fire, I saw the portly figure of Sam, the night-watchman. He waved cheerfully. If the Department of Employment had held selection tests to pick out a night-watchman for Pillings they could hardly have made a worse choice from Pillings' point of view. I often tried to imagine what the great efficiency expert Orwell Pilling would have made of Sam, if he really knew him. Sam believed in comfort and well being – it hadn't taken Ambrose and his friends more than one night's pleasant conversation to bring him into the camp. Now Sam was almost embarrassing in his efforts to help.

'Want any more jam, Ambrose,' he would say, poking his bald head round the corner. 'Happen to have noticed there's a new consignment.'

'How about some cheese? They've some lovely Stilton.'

Or, 'Fancy some hock from the Rhine district?'

Of course, it was all very immoral, no doubt – but by whose standards?

I was pondering on this curiously academic problem all the way up the stairs to the toy department.

'Sure, and here we are,' said Liam, with a flourish. He looked at me appraisingly.

'Hope you can play Monopoly?'

I was a bit taken aback.

'Monopoly? Well, yes, I have played once or twice.'

'Good,' Liam rubbed his hands. 'Then you can take Dick's place. He's had to go and do a job for Ambrose.'

He looked at his watch.

'We've an hour before supper. So come on.'

I sat down with the rest of them, Liam, Mr Grundy, Ann, Miss Starling, faces that had suddenly become familiar in my life. It was a little like working in a factory, or maybe being a member of the crew of a boat settling down for a long voyage – yes, that was it.

'Your throw,' said Mr Grundy.

I picked up the dice and threw, and began moving my counters around the Monopoly Board with its tantalising offers of Park Lane and Mayfair, or Railway Stations ... I was conscious that I was, indeed, embarking on a long voyage.

6

At seven-thirty we finished the game: at that stage white-haired Mr Grundy owned the best part of richer London, I had cornered three railway stations and Liam clung stubbornly to Pentonville Road.

'Pity,' said Mr Grundy, drily. 'Another half an hour and it would *all* be mine.'

He had a way of emphasising odd words, Mr Grundy.

'Time for a *proper* meal, I think,' he now said. And I remembered a previous conversation when he tapped me on the shoulder and remarked, '*Plenty* of time at Pillings, my boy.'

I supposed there was: but as I was now taken by Liam, who seemed to be my official guide for the evening, up to the men's wear department to dress suitably for dinner I couldn't help reflecting that time was pretty efficiently occupied.

However, I went on reflecting – as I dressed carefully in best quality white shirt, collar and black tie and evening dress suit (not for the first time in my life but for the first time for many years) – it was a pleasant enough way to occupy time.

That evening there were twelve of us sitting down to dinner at the long Jacobean type table provided by Messrs Pillings as one of the showpieces of their furnishing department, well tucked away from outside windows, and consequently discreetly lit by tall red candles in silver candlesticks.

I felt there should be one more diner, and looked inquiringly at Ambrose. He held his hands out expressively.

'Our friend Alfred has missed opening time again. I am

afraid he is often torn between the two choices of opening times.'

'In other words,' put in Liam, 'the old blarney has gone off on the booze and we shan't see him until tomorrow night.'

'That, my friend, is one of the few basic rules we must adhere to,' went on Ambrose. 'If we cannot be in the store before it closes then on no account come near it until the next day. There was once an unfortunate occasion when a member was delayed and chose to make an illicit attempt to force an entry and drew the attention of the police. It provided a rather stimulating night – too stimulating for our peace of mind.'

'Sure and it was a fine old how do you do,' said Liam jovially. 'We had the devil's own job to keep to ourselves ... 'Twas three hours before they called off the search.'

'So you can imagine we don't want any suspicion of that sort of trouble,' said Ambrose.

'No, of course not.'

'Well now,' went on Ambrose, reverting to his hostly role. 'What shall we drink tonight? Sherry? Hock? I hear there is some very delicious Riesling direct from Hungary ...'

'Sam?' I said.

Ambrose grinned.

'Sam indeed – great help, Sam.'

We had sherry first, the Riesling with the meal. The meal – ah, words can hardly do justice. There was a beautiful French onion soup with garlic, followed by creamed turbot and then mouth-watering lobster salad, and afterwards frozen raspberries and cream.

'You know,' said Mr Grundy seriously. 'The food here has improved a good deal since they fitted in that new type of deep freeze.'

It was the sort of meal which was impossible not to enjoy – which demanded whole-hearted concentration.

It was only at the end, as we sat back with popping eyes and swollen bellies that I ventured to broach my curiosity.

'Doesn't the food department notice any shortages?'

'What about the wines?'

'And the cheese ...?'

'Don't Pillings *ever* smell a rat?'

Ambrose leaned back.

'No ... and for a very good reason. Our organisation is planned entirely from the supposition – suppose Pillings guessed? What would make them guess? What is the best way of stopping them from even becoming suspicious? We always put ourselves in the position of Pillings, and then it is easier to answer the question.

'Take, for example, the matter of food. You may not be aware of it, but every day Pillings order 300 chickens. The daily intake of sausages runs into hundreds of pounds, bacon ditto, ham ditto. Cheese – why, they buy them in the rounds, roll after roll. Eggs – thousands of eggs, best quality, of course. Potatoes – possibly millions of potatoes in the year.

'Buying is in bulk, because it's cheaper that way. And so our veritable drops in the ocean are never noticed. But even so, we are very careful. The meal tonight was made up from two chickens – one removed yesterday, one today. An infinitesimal occurrence in an organisation of the size of Pillings, I can assure you.

'It's the same with wine, coffee, tea. Pillings buy crates of tea chests, several are always open, we take small quantities at a time ...'

Ambrose wagged a finger.

'However, feeding is only one aspect of the problem. We also have to clothe ourselves, find reading matter, writing ink, papers, perfumes for the ladies, shaving tackle for the men ... The clue to it all is moderation. The same applies to the members of our circle – we try always to keep our numbers within reason.'

'Yes,' put in Dick (I noticed everyone spoke freely and without hesitation, as they felt). 'Sometimes there's been a real queue waiting to get into Pillings.'

'Then how have I –?'

'You were lucky,' said Ambrose. 'This is a slack time of the year.'

Then, abruptly, he changed the subject. I had an uncomfortable feeling that he had decided it was time for a little reticence as far as I was concerned.

I could hardly blame him. After all, I had appeared out of the blue, and though maybe his intuition told him I was 'one of us', he was taking quite a risk. Come to think of it they must all take a phenomenal risk every time they admitted someone to their membership. For if just one person proved a squealer and split to the authorities ...

But nobody did, and nobody ever had; that was the surprising and very significant thing.

I talked about this with Eve, later that evening. We were all enjoying a little dance in the gramophone department. Liam and Dick had rolled back the carpet and someone had put on the automatic player, turned down discreetly, and we were jiving it up, round and round, to the latest rock and rolls and mambos. Ambrose danced with Miss Starling, Dick danced with Ann, and Liam and I took turns with Eve.

This was my turn, and I was enjoying it. She moved easily and supply in my arms, this woman who mystified me with her self-composure and withdrawn poise. I wondered about her a lot; but I decided to leave the probing of her background until later, and broached instead the problem of the complete security secrecy.

'It's not surprising,' said Eve, as we whirled round the small floor. 'You've heard of honour among thieves and all that?'

'Yes, but – well, do you really suggest that everyone who comes here is a thief?'

'In the eyes of the world, yes.'

'What does that mean?'

Eve laughed.

'I suppose it does sound melodramatic. No, I don't exactly mean each one of us would rob his or her own mother. But we are all on the other side of the fence, there's no doubt about that – else we wouldn't be here. We come here as a last resort – or, looked at in another way, as the first stage of something different.'

The dance came to an end; but we went on talking, leaning against the windows of one of the booths.

'I don't know about you,' said Eve, figuratively letting her hair down a little, so to speak. 'But until I came here I didn't really understand about people and relationships, about community spirit. The world I knew before was a little like – like a jungle. You just had to fight to exist. You didn't have much time to stop and worry whether you were hurting someone.'

She shrugged her smooth shoulders.

'I guess I was like that, too. I used to hurt people. And then one day I was hurt myself, badly. I felt it just couldn't go on – I wanted to commit suicide, to escape … That's about the time I came here.'

'But what brought you here?' I asked keenly. 'I mean, how did you know?'

'The answer to that one is – how did you know? You didn't … You just happened to find yourself here and the idea came to you why not stay here? That's what I mean about us being on the other side of the fence. The mass of the folk of this world, the sort that catch their tubes and buses to work every morning, and do this every Monday night, that every Tuesday night, and so on – they wouldn't do what we have done. Oh, yes, they might talk about it and dream about it, and they might say, if only we had the time, the money, the chance … but they haven't and they don't.'

I shrugged.

'Maybe we're just escapists.'

'Maybe.' Eve looked around at the happy little group. Ambrose was now whirling Ann round, Liam was dancing with Miss Starling – in a corner Mr Grundy was discussing something abstruse with Dick who, poor fellow, was trying hard to follow.

'But don't you think it's something rather more than mere escape?'

'Somehow I don't think it's quite the right word – escape, yes, but escape into life.'

We resumed our dance. We whirled round and round, now to a fast jazzy trumpet from the late-lamented Louis Armstrong. After a while the records changed, our partners changed. I danced with Ann – young, fresh, vivacious Ann, who had come here when she ran away from an unhappy home. Now she was working in the daytime with a veterinary surgeon.

'I love animals, don't you? Did you know there's a tropical fish bowl in the basement? I spend a lot of time there. Would you like to see?'

I nodded, and Ann looked pleased. She took me by the hand and led me down stairs, to where lights could be shown, and a game of table tennis was in progress.

The tropical fish were in the far end, floating about lazily, their wonderful colours making patterns that were fascinating to watch.

'Aren't they lovely? I'll give them some food.'

Ann reached over to a stack of fish food packets on one of Pillings' counters and lightly sprinkled some of the contents over the open water surface. We watched the fish dive upwards and snap at their unexpected meal.

'See how happy they are – everything provided for them.'

Ann gave me a mischievous glance, which confirmed me in my opinion that she deserved to go a long way.

Pillings had a few other pets for Ann's amusement. There were birds and parrots and some guinea pigs. The birds chirped away, there was something fresh and cheerful about their singing. Their music often seemed to swell up and fill the whole area with its happy sound.

We went over and watched the table tennis. When the others had finished, Ann and I had a knock up. Then we began to feel tired, and decided to go up again.

'You know,' I said thoughtfully, as we went upstairs. 'I had no idea that Pillings was such a happy place.'

It was, too. The Pillings that I came to know. Of course – it is rather different to the one you may know, in which there is a ceaseless rush from counter to counter, crowds everywhere, harassed shop assistants; on sales days positive chaos.

No, that is not *my* Pillings at all ...

My Pillings, as I came to know it during the ensuing weeks, was a haven, a microscopic world of its own – a world that began at 6 or so, and ended at 9 a.m. every morning. What happened outside those times was the outer, unreal world of Pillings – we were the inner, secret world. We were the true inhabitants, the users of Pillings – it was really for us that Pillings offered their famous value.

And what value it was, too. Exquisite meals, cooked on the latest electric stoves, washed down by the pick of an extensive wine list. Perfect comfort, relaxing in the most expensive foam rubber armchairs or studio couches with contemporary elongated legs ... Slumberland mattresses for sleeping on – modern equipment for playing games – the latest television and radio sets – a full range of fashions in the ladies department and ditto for the men – even the facilities of a modern hairdressing salon with only one minor drawback that you had to get your friends to do the cutting and trimming. Variety on every floor, and on a balmy summer evening, the fragrant scented pathways of the roof garden.

I mean to say, what more could anyone ask? I found that, willy-nilly – scruples or no scruples – I settled down into the comfortable routine. It *was* a sort of routine, even though most pleasant. But we broke it up as much as possible. Monday night was television night, there was usually a good play. Tuesday was more of a reading night, most of us took a new book out of the up-to-date Pillings' library and settled down in comfort. Wednesday night was something of a social get-together, we would dress up a bit and have something of a celebration (it was one of these nights, appropriately, when I made my entry into Pillings). Thursday was games night – table tennis, skittles, billiards, and so on – I soon discovered a partiality for Chinese checkers, and had many hectic battles with Ambrose.

It was during one of these that I returned to the subject of

Pillings and its founder.

'What sort of man is this Orwell Pilling?'

Ambrose executed a deft movement, getting home a piece.

'Oh, well ... one can only surmise, of course. Astute, practical, far-seeing in a way, very efficient in his approach to things – a man who built something from nothing, you might say.'

I made a smaller, less successful move. As I did so I reflected that Ambrose, too, had many of these qualities. And suddenly I thought of the simile of opposites being alike.

'I suppose in a way you feel you are outwitting Pilling himself, with all this?'

Ambrose smiled.

'I wouldn't like to say that ... one can never be certain.' He hesitated, and then went on with a curious, almost diffident smile. 'Besides, he is a clever man ... so I understand.'

I found myself often thinking about Orwell Pilling, the sort of fountainhead of this vast empire. I wondered what sort of man he was, to have devoted a life to creating such a humming dome – and what he would think or say if he knew just what went on when darkness fell. I had a sneaking suspicion that he might be rather intrigued.

But as I was saying – Friday night was writing night, when we would sit in the big spacious writing room kindly provided by Pillings for the convenience of customers, and on their cream-tinted notepaper, provided free, we would conduct our weekly correspondence with mothers and fathers, brothers and sisters and other dear ones. The only difference between us and Pillings' regular customers was that we used to nip over into the sub-post office and 'borrow' stamps for our letters.

Saturday night was the weekly management meeting, a fairly serious occasion when we planned the next week's programmes, discussed any problems that might have arisen and so on. 'Any other business' ranged over a wide field, from whether we dared to snaffle yet another bottle of Haig whisky to the possible dangers of taking theatre tickets booked through the shop's theatre department. Sometimes we spent long periods gravely deciding what might seem quite trivial points; but gradually I came to see that perhaps they were not trivial, for in the discussion we were proving in some way, our right to be called a true community.

Sunday night was the quietest of all. We sat back and relaxed and talked gently, remembering the days before we all became – well, shall I say, more enlightened.

'Strange,' said Liam lazily one night, as we sat with our feet stretched out before one of the latest eletrically-operated mock fire-places. 'I used to work quite hard doing what I didn't want to do. Now I don't have to worry about food and a roof over my head, or anything else for that matter.'

He grinned disarmingly.

'Pity of it is, I still don't do anything else!'

But others made better use of their time. Miss Starling had taken up painting. She borrowed one of the new kits from the art department, set up her easel, and produced some interesting still lifes. She was now working on a portrait of Eve which I liked very much, and had determined somehow to buy.

Dick was something of a craftsman with models, he was always building model motor cars. Liam was something of a photographer, and with the aid of an abundant equipment from the photography department at Pillings he was able to do some interesting indoor work, and had even won prizes at several exhibitions. The stocky man with glasses, Max, was a craftsman of a different kind, he made copper work, and had reached such a proficiency that had recently achieved something of a record – he now came and visited the buyer at Pillings in the daytime and was given handsome orders to produce copper work from materials which he carefully filched from the same store by night.

Mr Grundy seemed to be about the only member besides Liam with no craft of his own. But in time I discovered that he, too, had a special vocation. Mr Grundy studied the markets. Every evening he settled down with the *Financial Times* and burrowed away. Sometimes his voice, slightly perturbed, would inform us:

'Bad show –Pillings down a half, Barkers and Selfridges both steady.'

Mr Grundy took a bird's-eye-view of the finances of the big store world. Nothing escaped his eagle eye, and he seemed to know about impending mergers before the administrators themselves.

'Well, Mr Grundy,' I said, one day, 'supposing I had the money, which store would you advise me to invest in?'

Mr Grundy looked at me in astonishment.

'Why, my boy, there can be no question, surely. Pillings, of course.'

Then he winked broadly.

'Pillings always give value for money.'

7

And so life might have gone on ... and on ... and on ... Had it not been for the startling announcement we read one evening in the paper – of a takeover bid by a large financial group for Pillings Store. Even then it wasn't so much the news of the takeover that caused alarm and despondency as a subsequent paragraph:

'A spokesman for the new owners stated today that among various administrative changes there will be a severe tightening up of security arrangements ...'

'I wonder what that means?' said Eve uneasily.

'It means,' said Ambrose, appearing on the scene, 'the introduction of an ex-Scotland Yard detective famed for his prowess in criminal investigation – I had the information today from a, er, reliable source. A gentleman by the name of MacTravers whose one aim will be to root us all out.'

'Trouble?' I said.

Ambrose nodded.

'Trouble.'

And yet again as he nodded in a curious way I had the

impression that he remained unworried – as if Ambrose would have an answer to this as he seemed to have for every contingency.

I first saw Joseph MacTravers two evenings later. In between we had waited on tenterhooks for his first move, almost disappointed when it didn't come. Then, as perhaps he had anticipated, we relaxed a little.

That was the time he chose for his first visit. I was on guard at the time. This involved keeping a watch on the swing doors from the ground floor, so that we had plenty of warning of an enemy approach.

This, I sensed at once, was a true enemy approach. MacTravers was a large, solid, dour-looking man, indeed in many ways the textbook outline of a detective. He had sandy, untidy hair, going thin, and wore a crumpled lounge suit, and carried in his hand a large silver torch. As yet there was no need for him to use the torch, but I imagined he had it all ready for probing into unsuspecting corners.

I guessed that this was in the nature of a little personal preview. He was the sort of man who would have a hunch: probably he had developed a strong one that something was not as it should be at Pillings. Maybe he had taken a look through the stock records, and found some discrepancies.

I frowned to myself, thinking that if there were, why hadn't these been noticed before?

Before I could develop this line of thought MacTravers came beefily and solidly down the long aisle, and it was time for me to crawl silently away along my prepared exits, to warn the others of impending danger.

We had worked out a very thorough technique, what we called our avoiding contact routine. We knew every inch of Pillings, better I suppose than anyone, certainly better than a newcomer like MacTravers. We knew where the linoleum rolls were as thick as a forest, where the thick piles of mattresses offered excellent protection, where stacks of tables blocked the view, where thick Persian draperies made it impossible to detect silent movements across even thicker Persian carpets.

Long ago we had decided on a very simple method of avoiding inquisitive intruders – retreat. We would simply retreat round and round Pillings store for as long as humanly possible. Barring ill luck we were convinced we could get away with it.

This was our first serious test. As soon as I had slipped upstairs to warn our comrades, we jumped into action. While two of us quickly obliterated all signs of our immediate presence, the rest of us began retreating to the next floor.

By the time the ponderous footsteps of MacTravers reached the second floor, we were on the third floor: and after he had rooted around the second and was on his way to the third, we were moving up to the fourth.

And so it went on. Like wraiths in the night we slipped quietly backwards and upwards, backwards and upwards – knowing always that we had both the rear and front stairs at our disposal when we wanted them – and that at the bottom, waiting for us, was no more serious symbol of authority than Sammy, the night-watchman.

Yes, it was almost amusing, that first time. I don't quite know why MacTravers had chosen to come on his own, but he had. Now and then, in the course of our retreat, I padded silently away from the others, and by climbing over soft beddings and furnishing and trailing through thick rows of curtains, I was able to get behind him, yet close enough to watch his reactions. He seemed to be a little uncertain, almost as if he was troubled by more than the immediate problem – as if in fact he was not quite sure what he should be doing.

When MacTravers came to the top floor, silently we had fled down to the basement. I presume at that stage he did not know we were there, that he had not uncovered any clues. We were in time at the bottom to have a quick word with Sammy who confirmed that MacTravers had come in quite casually, announcing his intention of having a stroll round.

As we spoke, we looked at one another worriedly. It was hard to believe that there would not soon be a time when

MacTravers came back – not alone.

But at least it was not to be this night. A little while later, by when we had spread upwards again, we heard the lift buzzing as he went down to the basement again, and a low murmur of voices as he conferred with Sammy.

Then at last there was silence, and we had Pillings to ourselves again.

But somehow, after that evening, we never felt that we really did. There was always an uneasiness in the air, a sense of uncertainty, we were always listening for the expected footsteps.

Meantime the events of the outside world seemed in an odd way to be running against our luck as well. We read in the newspapers that there were to be large re-organisations at Pillings, and that on the new board it was unlikely that there would be a place for the former managing director, Mr Orwell Pilling.

'Funny,' said Mr Grundy, stroking the tip of his nose reflectively. 'I've grown quite fond of old Orwell.'

Ambrose looked at him with a smile.

'Old? How do you know he's old?'

'Oh, must be. All these financial wizards are. I used to be in that side of things you know. Never met any successful City birds that were a day under sixty.'

'Well,' said Eve, 'that's not so very old, anyway, these days.'

'Course not,' said Dick. 'I often sell cars to men of sixty – reckless fellows, too, some of them are, fair menace on the road.'

'Well, anyway,' said Mr Grundy, 'I'm sorry to read this.'

He turned to Ambrose.

'You know, it seems to me that things are going from grey to black.'

I nodded.

'I agree. What do you think?'

I watched Ambrose curiously. He didn't seem unhappy. No, he seemed – well, resigned was more the word. He had worn for some days now a curious look of such resignation. It puzzled me, but I could not find the explanation.

'Yes, things are black.' He shrugged. 'I suppose they'll get blacker ... But then what can we do? It's out of our hands ...'

No doubt that was not a very appropriate banner with which to enter into battle: It's out of our hands ... Yet that was the main feeling we experienced after that day. I felt in some way in the grip of events beyond my control, that my hiding among the linoleum rolls was no longer going to make any difference in the end.

And curiously, this foreknowledge led an added sweetness to our last two or three days. I remember in particular one evening walking with Eve in our beloved roof-garden, holding hands, and talking about our first meeting.

'I used to think you aloof and unreal,' I said.

'Perhaps I was. Perhaps we all are – unreal, I mean. We are always surrounded by shadows ...'

I knew what she meant, that perhaps we might disappear into those shadows.

'And yet,' I said, 'we have done no real harm. It's not as if we were cruel, or malicious, or making war, or inventing atom bombs, or subjugating other people.'

Eve smiled.

'We've done worse than that – we've gone against the moral code. Thou shalt not steal, even if it's from Pillings' abundant larder.'

I couldn't really feel guilty about that. Not any longer. Not after I had learned something about the real suffering in the world.

Then at last came the night we had been expecting. It was a dark, storm-brewing night. Looking out of a window, late, we noticed a large black car drive up, and several men getting out in police uniform.

I went and told Ambrose. He nodded.

'I've been expecting them.'

So had we all. But Ambrose, I noticed, said it almost as if – yes, almost as if he really had been expecting them, this evening. I shrugged. I did not fully understand Ambrose, but I was not surprised if he did know a great deal more than I did about these things. He was a very wise man.

For a time there was no more disturbance: the men had come into the building, the doors closed, and then silence. But soon they would come up the stairs.

I was glad by now it was dark, then I thought – of course they will switch on the lights.

'Can't we cut off the lights?' I said.

'It's done,' said Ambrose quietly. He looked at me with an almost mischievous gleam in his eyes.

'You know I think this is going to be rather amusing.'

We waited for the sound of footsteps; and at last we heard them coming, thud-thud-thud. Now we heard the flick of light switches, and one or two exclamations as the darkness remained.

Then as they reached the first floor we saw the lights of their torches stabbing through the darkness.

'Watch carefully,' whispered Ambrose. 'You see that although it's a bright light, it's rather glaring, only lighting up the small patch. Provided we have enough protection we should be safe. We must be like chameleons, taking on the appearance of our surroundings.'

All at once, Ambrose seemed very young and lively. It was as if in the sudden action of the evening he was shedding all other worries and responsibilities. Now he took charge of things, ordering us about, rather like the leader of a boy scout movement. Mr Grundy was detailed to cover our flank, with Ann to help him, and I was to take Eve and Dick to the top of the rear stairs, while Ambrose and Sammy and the others remained, as Ambrose put it, 'mobile'. Their job was to detract attention away from us.

'But remember, if at all possible we want to outlast them,' said Ambrose, suddenly grave.

Having scoured the first floor, the police party now came up to the second. We watched their shadowy figures outlined against the glass doorways. One bulkier and more formidable than the others, we knew, must be out pet tracker, MacTravers.

When they came in a blast of cool air came in with them and filtered around the store. I was with Eve behind a double-tiered stand. Suddenly one of the torches swept around the room. I felt it all around us, and we pressed ourselves deep into the shadows. For a moment the torch wavered, and then it passed on. We watched its prodding journey, over the huge divans behind which crouched Dick, on and around the garden furniture which hid Eve; on and on until it reached the other end of the floor, where Mr Grundy and company were ensconced in wardrobes.

It was then, as the torch wavered uncertainly and then went out, that we were startled to hear the voice of MacTravers:

'Now then – are you listening to me? I know you're there – I *know*.'

He repeated with emphasis his knowledge. He assured us he knew all about us, he produced a few facts to show that he had at least collected some evidence of our existence.

'Somewhere in this place you're hiding, and sooner or later we're going to find you – so come on, now, give yourselves up.'

His only answer was silence. I could hardly even hear myself breathe.

'Very well,' said MacTravers. 'In that case, we'll search every inch until we find you. Come on, lads.'

I leaned over and pressed Eve's hand reassuringly. Silently we began our retreat to the next floor, slipping like well trained shadows through the darkness. By the time MacTravers had marshalled his men into a complicated criss-cross routine, we had moved to the next floor altogether.

'Listen,' said Ambrose, materialising like a ghost. 'We must keep absolutely still. I think it's time we took up position C, as we rehearsed.'

I hesitated. Position C meant hiding effectively until the searchers had passed us by and gone on to the next floor. It was something we had practised, but never, so to speak, performed.

Ambrose sensed my doubts.

'The truth is,' he said simply, 'we have to do something drastic or we will be caught. They mean business.'

We split up hastily, and searched for our bedrock hiding places. It's strange how hard it is to really obliterate yourself when it comes to it. Cupboard, wardrobes, chests, none of them seem half as safe on examination.

Eve and I had previously decided on the safest place of all; in the kitchen department were several rows of dustbins, nearly thirty in all. It was unlikely, we felt, that the police would imagine them to be populated by human beings, or bother to search them.

Now we sank silently into a dustbin each, leaving the lids slightly ajar for air.

Soon we heard footsteps of the searchers. Suddenly they seemed to be all around us, great thundering movements. I crouched low, wishing I could hold Eve's hand. I suddenly felt conscious of my weakness, vulnerability. I could have sworn they were passing down the dustbins, perhaps opening them one by one. Nearer and nearer they came, until I was sure that I buried my head in my hands and closed my eyes and hoped for the best.

And then, abruptly, they were gone.

I waited a while, and then cautiously raised my lid. Almost as if moved by a physic impulse, Eve raised her lid, and we stared at each other through the darkness. Quickly I put my hand out and touched Eve's.

'They're gone,' I whispered. 'We'll just wait a while and –'

Suddenly my words were cut across by a commotion on the floor above, and then a wild shout.

'Goodness – ' began Eve.

We listened, all kinds of thoughts flooding through our minds – but, predominantly, the knowledge: it's happened at last.

Apparently, as we later found out, they came across Mr Grundy, who had not hidden himself with quite so much efficiency as the rest of us.

All was now confusion. We decided the best thing now the alarm had been given, would be to go up to the next floor and distract the police from chasing the members they had trapped up there.

When we got there torches were flashing everywhere, and by their light we caught a glimpse first of the police, and then of the fleeting, ghostly figure of Mr Grundy, followed by Ann.

Ambrose was somewhere. His voice rang out strongly:

'Keep moving, Mr G. Keep moving. Help is on the way – strong reinforcements coming.'

I knew from the tone of his voice that he was indulging in a complete flight of fancy, but of course the police wouldn't be aware of that. They seemed startled to hear Ambrose's voice, and at once swung round to train their torches in the direction it had come from – but of course by then he was far away.

Now began the fantastic chase. I don't know whether at the back of his mind Ambrose had always planned something like this, if the worst came to the worst. But suddenly he called us all to him, and told us to make a mad rush through the stores.

'Jump – leapfrog – anything,' he whispered. 'At all costs keep moving – and don't forget – pull things down as you go.'

We took him literally. We leaped and jumped, and pulled things down – lampstands, shelves, counters – we went through the furnishing departments like a tornado, so familiar with the layout that we had no need of torches.

The policemen chasing us were not so fortunate. As we pulled down things behind us, so they ran straight into them, falling over and sprawling headlong, with loud cries and groans.

By the time we reached the doors they were floundering about helplessly.

'Now we must split up,' hissed Ambrose. 'Half up, half down. And remember – keep moving. And the ones at the top – you come down the back stairs, and we'll rendezvous in the basement.'

Before we had time to reflect on the rights or wrongs of his advice the torches were flickering about again. Eve and I, along with Dick and Ann, went to the linoleum department. As we were chased into the room it was an easy matter to send the long rolls sliding down, so that our followers were sent sprawling, and one by one the torches went out. If you have ever tried to climb up among moving rolls of glossy linoleum, you have some idea of their difficulties.

Soon we had reached the doors, and after fighting off a natural desire to seek sanctuary on the roof-garden, which would in fact have been a fatal cul-de-sac, we went flying down the rear stairs. On the way down we saw a torch coming up to meet us, so we slid through the swing doors on to the second floor, there to jump from one bed to another, covering a fantastic distance in a short time. Indeed I could not help thinking, as we soared through the air, that if we had had the foresight to provide ourselves with spring pads, perhaps we could have leaped our way right out of the store.

However, we were at least well ahead of our pursuers, and fled on, down through the food and wine departments, down and down to the basement.

Here we were met by Sammy.

'Ambrose says to keep up the chase as long as we can, but if we feel things are going against us – he means if there's a danger of us really being caught – then we must all make for the door marked "Third Store Room".'

I paused, confused.

'Surely there isn't –?'

But there was no time to query further. Sammy raced off in one direction, Eve and I in another. We flitted from side to side through the darkness, while the tramping feet and probing torches came after us.

In fact, it became rather like a fantastic ballet in the shadows, the ballet of our farewell to Pillings. By now I could see no end to things but our arrest and disgrace. I felt that we were even now devouring our last few minutes of freedom.

And then, suddenly, feeling this, I caught something of Ambrose's mood of careless defiance, and plunged back into the chase.

Backwards and forwards, up from one floor to another, then down again – so it went on. At one stage I believe there were some of us on every floor, and we were all, in a perverse sort of way, enjoying ourselves in a return to the days of schoolboy adventures.

But all the time I was aware that we were just buying time, that sooner or later they would bring reinforcements, would get the lights working, would –

'Darling,' whispered Eve at last. 'It's time we went to the basement and looked for that door.'

We flitted down, and somehow gathered together all the others. By using our expert knowledge of the geography of the store, we managed momentarily to leave the police floundering on the ground floor.

Ambrose was waiting down there.

'What now?' I said, out of breath.

With a quick movement Ambrose pulled us to a corner of the basement, to the store-room doors. I had thought they were always permanently locked, but to my surprise he now produced a key and inserted it into the door marked 'Third Store-Room'. With a push it swung open, and Ambrose switched on the light.

It was quite a small room, but in the far corner was a single, closed door.

'Through there,' hissed Ambrose. 'You'll find a corridor – follow it as far as you can until you come to another door. Open that – and you'll find yourself – well, somewhere familiar, and pretty safe. Only hurry, for goodness sake, hurry.' His voice broke a little, and he said quickly: 'And the best of luck!'

'But – ' Eve's voice reflected our consternation. 'Aren't you coming?'

Ambrose shook his head.

'No ... but please don't worry. I shall be quite all right.'

I felt I wanted to say something: where would we meet again, how would we meet – but suddenly there was the sound of returning police.

'Quick,' hissed Ambrose. 'What do you want – freedom or prison?'

And he half pushed us across to the doorway, bundling us through the opening, and clicking the door closed after us.

We stood there, almost petrified. On the other side of the door we could imagine the scene, the policemen pounding up, shining their torches. Surely Ambrose would be exposed, seen – caught?

We listened anxiously. But there was no commotion, no sounds of struggle, just nothing. Just the footsteps coming – and then stopping, and then going away again. Had Ambrose vanished into nothing? Or ... what?

I took Eve by the hand.

'Well ... let's do as Ambrose said.'

We went along the corridor. It was a long, long corridor, and our journey seemed exceptionally sad and endless. But at last we came to the door Ambrose had told us about, and when we opened it, we found ourselves, miraculously, out in the High Street – and safety.

8

It is difficult to remember, in retrospect, just how we spent the remainder of that night. Mostly, we felt suddenly lost, rudderless, without direction: as if we were children whose parents had been whisked away, forever. Forever ... a terrible word: but only so long as you believe in it. At first, I know, we were all overcome by this sense of blank despair. Bewilderment, too. I, for one, could not make head or tail of that last moment development. How had we escaped? How had Ambrose known about the door? How – there were questions spinning round in my head, round and round.

I remember we sat in an all-night cafe, drinking coffee, and speaking much, looking sometimes at one another as if seeing for the first time who we were ... down and outs, destitute, the lost and damned ...

It was all wrong, I felt it in my bones. It was not the right way to be thinking. Life offers always the choice between hope and despair. We had all of us once known despair and we had been given the great gift of hope. We should not throw it away too lightly.

I leaned over to Mr Grundy.

'Well?'

'My dear fellow, after my recent harrowing experiences I cannot think clearly. I can only contemplate the ruins and the disintegration of my former paradisical existence – amen!'

I shook Mr Grundy by the shoulder.

'You mustn't say that. Ambrose wouldn't want us to think like that.'

'Ambrose?' said Mr Grundy, with mock indifference. 'Who is Ambrose?' He sighed. 'Now there is no one in the world but streets and unfriendly houses, policemen, the law ...'

'That's not so.'

'What's your alternative?' said Dick, keenly. He spread his hands out expressively. 'We're together now, at the moment. But unless you have some alternative, we're going to go our own ways. And then – why it's almost as if we've never been together.'

'Ah, no,' said Mr Grundy wisely. 'I don't think that is strictly true. I think we must all agree ...'

He went on with an elaborate dissertation on the benefits that we had all derived from our strange communal life, but most of the time I was only half listening. I kept thinking back, to the experiences of a few hours previously. I kept trying to put the pieces together: for there was a puzzle there, a problem – and maybe I would understand a lot of things if I could fit it altogether.

In the end things bothered me so much that I decided to take Eve for a walk. We arranged to meet the others at tea-time; by then we could have come to some decision.

We walked for a time in silence. Eve guessed that I was trying to work things out, and she kept silent. At the same time I was pleasantly conscious of her walking beside me, looking cool and unruffled for all her hectic adventures. It was strange how much in unison we had become: difficult to believe that a short while ago we did not know of one another's existence. That at least was something that Pillings had achieved; our happiness.

Pillings ... I kept coming back to that name, to that place. I wondered, as I had so often wondered, why Ambrose had picked on it in the first place. Had it been pure chance? Or had there been a reason?

My mind switched away again, back to the door ... that unknown, half hidden door. Who had put it there? Who had planned an escape like that? How could Ambrose have known?

'Well,' said Eve at last. 'Solved the mystery?'

I shrugged.

'Who said there was a mystery?'

'You know there is. And, what's more, you won't be happy till you've solved it. So go ahead – what's the solution?'

It wasn't what Eve said, so much as her use of the word, mystery, that started me off on the right track. There was not, apparently any real mystery – last night had just been the inevitable process, the police had come searching for us, and they had caught up with us – at least, they had nearly caught up with us, but thanks to Ambrose – and *that* was the mystery. How had Ambrose *known*?

I stopped in my tracks suddenly.

'Now what?'

'What's the time?' I said urgently.

'Just gone ten, I heard a clock strike. Why?'

Ten. Yes, that should be late enough, I reckoned.

'Come on ... We've an appointment.'

I have always, as I may have remarked, been a great believer in hunches. It was a hunch that took me into Pillings those long months ago, a hunch that made me stay, a hunch that made me do many things in life I might not otherwise have done.

Now this hunch carried me along on the wave of its

urgency, across the park, through another park, on to a bus and all the way to that busy street dominated by the great glaring sign: PILLINGS – THE SUPER STORE. It even got me through the swing doors and into the usual morning bustle of shoppers, before I began to lose a little confidence.

'Darling ... ' whispered Eve, 'what on earth?'

I looked around, surprised to see that there was little evidence of last night's rumpus. Strange, I thought, that there was so little sign ... and that there had been nothing in the papers, either. One would have thought ...

I made up my mind to follow out my hunch.

'Darling, don't ask any questions, just follow me – and don't be afraid.'

I took Eve by the hand and led her up stairs, up past the entrances to the first and second floors, up and up until we came to the rather forbidding notice: Administrative Offices.

We went past this, up to the office counter and the secretary waiting with the polite expression. I hesitated, then looked past her quickly to the neat labelled rows of offices: Sales Director, Chief Buyer, Publicity Manager ... I noticed, almost detachedly, that a workman was standing before a door at the end, painting over the lettering on the glass. I read the last five letters of the last word, and suddenly knew that my hunch must be right.

'Come on, Eve!'

Quickly, ignoring the secretary's vague cry of protest, I pulled Eve after me, running across and bursting straight through the door that still bore the remnants of that once proud emblem: ORWELL PILLING, Managing Director.

He was in the middle of tidying up the papers on his desk, filing them away into brief cases, clearing up the labours of a lifetime even as the man on the door finished obliterating his nameplate. As we burst in he turned and looked up.

'Ambrose!' cried Eve.

'Ambrose ... ' I repeated, rather weakly.

He gave us a warm, welcoming smile; not half as sad as I had expected.

'Hullo, you two. I thought perhaps you might come. An intelligent couple.'

Eve looked in bewilderment from Ambrose to me.

'But I had no idea –'

Ambrose smiled at me inquiringly. I shrugged.

'When you showed us that door. You had it all off so pat – I thought then, there could only be one person who would know – one other person. And then it suddenly all clicked into place.'

'Yes,' said Ambrose. He opened his mouth as if about to launch into a wordy explanation: then paused and went over to the door. He said something to the man outside, and then came in, closing the door firmly behind him.

'After all, I might as well enjoy my last hour or two here in the comparative peace to which I am accustomed.'

'But Ambrose,' began Eve again, indicating the plushy room, the contemporary, expensive furniture. 'Why – how –?'

Ambrose settled back in the swivel chair, and motioned us to be comfortable.

'Have a cigar? Cigarette? Remember – it's on the house!' As he spoke, I saw him for a moment as the old Ambrose again.

'Don't joke!' said Eve, almost reproachfully.

Ambrose nodded, and held up a chiding hand.

'It's true, my dear, that you are witnessing the uncovering of the mystery – it's true that I am Orwell Pilling. But, then again, it's just as true that I am Ambrose. You see – well, it's a long story, and perhaps I can put the succinct facts simplest by suggesting to you that in every one of us there are really two people – call them if you will, good and bad, rogue and saint, black and white.

'My trouble, frankly, is that for too many years I was just one person – Orwell Pilling, businessman and prig, self-seeking tycoon, ruthless administrator, etc. etc. – the man in fact who built up this business which now, alas, falls into even more unscrupulous hands.'

'But Ambrose,' said Eve softly. 'That's nothing to be

terribly ashamed of – I mean, a strong business is a good business, I suppose.'

Ambrose Orwell Pilling looked doubtful.

'That is as may be. It is, alas, not any concern of mine after today. But the point I wanted to make has nothing to do with the quality of my business, but of the man who made it, *me*. In the process, as I came to discover, I made myself into a person of whom I became more and more ashamed. And so –'

'The person inside you revolted?' I said.

Ambrose smiled.

'Correct. I used to come in to the store every morning at nine o'clock precisely. I was always far more punctual than any of my staff, and I used to despise them all – and I would pace around, finding fault here and there, issuing orders like any tin god dictator, then retiring here to my official sanctum, only to spend the time issuing even more edicts. Oh, it was all quite unreal, I can see that now. And then when I had done all that, there was really nothing left for me to do except perhaps to take a walk on the roof garden and think, well, I'm the king of the castle – so what? It was then ...'

He paused, got up and walked over to the window, turning and standing with his back to the light, so that he became faintly shadowy in outline: so that he might very well have been Orwell Pilling or Ambrose – or both.

' ... that I became interested in the obverse side of the coin. I thought, it's all very well, I know how I live and how I cope with my problems, but how does someone live who is not powerful and in charge of a vast business, what are his problems and how does he cope? Soon the thought became an obsession with me ... and in the end, being I suppose a man of some determination, I felt I must put it to the test. So one night I dressed up in some very old clothes, slipped out of my house by the back entrance – and went on the tramp.

'I did this for several nights, and I can tell you I was always glad when I came home and crept into a nice soft bed. But then my conscience began to trouble me further. I told myself, just supposing I had no soft bed to return to, no warm food waiting ... supposing I had nowhere to go, no roof over my head?

'This led me to the inevitable testing of that theory. And from that it wasn't long before I came into the general state of mind which no doubt encouraged you two to make your first illicit entry into the world of Pillings. By then I had acquired one or two companions – Sammy, for example – we used to tramp about together ... And when we were thinking about where to get a good night's sleep and the idea came about one of the stores – well, I must confess the coincidence proved irresistible, and I said – "Why not make it Pillings?"

'The strange thing is,' went on Ambrose, returning to his swivel chair and swinging slowly from side to side with just a touch of the old managing director. 'The more I went on with what was admittedly a sort of game to start with – the less of a game it became. I found myself meeting other men and women with no homes, no money, nothing to eat, few clothes – little or no hope. I began to realise that the world was a very different place for them – that for every one Orwell Pilling, there were thousands like this. I came to see that sitting in my centrally heated office, waited on by a lot of lackeys, I was cut off from the real humanity of the world. And so, I began to realise – so were too many people in this country – cut off from their fellows, cut off from appreciating the real factors of living ...'

Ambrose shrugged.

'From then on, it was a question of educating myself. I came to understand many things, just as you two have done. To put it in a nutshell, I became aware that the world is nothing, if we do not all of us take an equal responsibility. The rest you know ...'

There was a sudden silence. In the middle of this came a tap on the door, and the workman poked his head round.

'Shall I get on with the job now, Mr Pilling?'

Ambrose looked from Eve to me, and then at the workman, and suddenly gave a loud laugh.

'Yes, yes, get on with the job – speed the parting guest on his way.'

Akwardly, we rose to our feet.

'Well — ' said Eve.

'We were wondering … ' I began. 'I mean, what will happen now? Is it all over?'

The look on the face of Ambrose Orwell Pilling was an incredulous one. He jumped to his feet, almost angrily.

'All over? My dear friends, it is most certainly *not* all over. Goodness me, we're just beginning.'

Quickly he reached for his hat, plonked it on his head, and then put an arm round each of us and walked us towards the door.

'Let's go for a little stroll, shall we? There are quite a few ideas I want to discuss with you two. Now, you probably know that I've been bought out of things here. Well, it's sad, but there it is … At least I've got a reasonable bit of capital – enough in fact –'

Ambrose pressed the button for the lift and ushered us in. He clicked the gates, and we began sinking downwards.

'Well, as a matter of fact, do you know what I had in mind? There's a big new store being built up the road – they say it will be one of the largest and most modern in the West Country. They say it will be able to provide the customer with every requirement from the cradle to the grave.'

Ambrose paused and gave a chuckle.

'I rather like that, don't you? "From the cradle to the grave" … Mmmh, yes, well, it seems to me that perhaps …'

The lift halted on the ground floor, and arm in arm the three of us walked across the marbled floor and out – for the last time – of Pillings.

'Where to now?' I asked, as we stood undecided on the edge of the ceaseless bustle of the busy street.

But Ambrose was hardly listening. Already he was peering, eyes agleam, up the street to where high above most of the other buildings reared the imposing new shape of the latest departmental store. Following his excited gaze we stared open-mouthed, our eyes dazzled, our minds full of new illuminations. At last we stirred.

'Forward!' cried Ambrose.

71

And happily we advanced upon our latest and greatest objective – the identity of which, for reasons which I am sure the reader will sympathetically understand, must forever remain a secret.

II

At The Rainbow's End

From the railway the cottage was clearly discernible; grey and
solid, the granite walls covered with creeping ivy and faded
moss, tucked under the brow of a Cornish hill. Sometimes a
passenger on the London-Penzance express, glancing idly out
of the window, might capture a brief but vivid portrait of a
whole mysterious life. The neat vegetable garden, the child's
bicycle, the man's underwear fluttering from the clothesline,
the half-glimpsed woman's face peering from behind lace
curtains, blue smoke curling out of the chimney pot as if to
underline the reality of existence – it was all revealed, almost
flaunted, before the casual gaze of passing travellers. But from
any other approach, the cottage was a world apart, a hidden
and secret place; three miles from the village and almost a
mile from the nearest habitation, a farm down the valley –
reached only by a wandering path across fields and woods,
and shrouded almost to the last moment by overgrown hedges
and bushes. A solitary and rather ugly sort of place where few
people would have chosen to live.

The woman had come there casually, without thinking.
Time, five years of it, had enabled her to develop a proper,
fierce hatred of its implacable solitude. As a child of twelve she
had been evacuated to the village after both her parents had
been killed in London's air-raids. Brought up by a strict,
disciplinarian foster-mother she had seized what seemed the
first opportunity of escape by marrying a man almost twice

her age, head cowman at one of the biggest farms in the district. He was Cornish, and carried about him the dark, romantic presence of the Celtic race. He was a big, strong man whose physical presence had stirred some fire deep down in her. At his touch her virgin fears were swept aside by strange passions she had not imagined. When he kissed her she had burned with a desire to obliterate herself into his body. She trembled at the thought of belonging to him, of being his slave, his plaything. The idea appealed to her instincts which were native to the sophisticated world of cities and so responded more excitedly to a dramatic conception of the wild, primitive life.

But when it was too late, the deed done, she realised she had cultivated an illusion. The cottage was a grave, her husband the undertaker. There was not even the compensation of some erotic personal life. His body, strong and exciting as it was to her, was directed by a mind both simple and unimaginative. He took her as he would a meal or a drink, satisfying his appetite in a whirlwind of crude passion which ended just as her own began to rise. That done, he lay back and fell into deep sleep, his face untroubled as a child's, but rendered curiously repulsive by a persistent snore. In the morning he was up at five o'clock, moving about heavily by the light of a paraffin lamp, dressing himself in the stout corduroys and thick shirts that smelled always of the farmyard. By dawn he was gone on the mile walk to his farm and she was left with the emptiness of her day – such emptiness that she was pathetically glad when she saw his stolid form returning across the fields in the evening. Yet after a few minutes she was appalled again at his limitations, his lack of conversation, of interest in anything beyond the farm, the weather, his own comforts.

The only time she discovered in him some original emotion was after the birth of their child. She awoke from a deep sleep after the birth to find him standing staring down at the baby. He looked at her with a face full of pride and happiness. 'It's a boy, then?' he said, and there was a curious satisfaction in his voice. But later, as the months and then the years began to pass, she realised that it was no more than momentary vanity that moved him; when that was done with he simply regarded the child as some object in his life, as necessary to the day as food, clothes, herself, the farm – no more.

After that she withdrew into herself, shutting out everything that reminded her of her plight; her husband, her child, the nearby village. She hardly ever went out, and when she did she felt alien and unhappy and hurried home as fast as she could to the remoteness of the cottage. At home, too, she gave up the struggle, becoming untidy and downright slovenly through lack of interest, so that soon they had continual rows about it, for he was a man of tidy mind and habits, as befitted a good countryman. She was not of the country. She knew that only too well. As if in protest she deliberately slopped about the place, encouraging everything to grow dirty and unkempt – even herself. Her prettiness became almost plain, her eyes dulled, her hair grew wild and fuzzy, her walk had the heaviness of despair. Only her body remained unchanged; strong and resilient, the breasts swelling to roundness, the skin soft and downy to the touch – a body shaped for passion, and kept alive by some flickering flame of secret desire whose gratification was beyond the conception, or caring, of her stolid husband.

To alleviate her misery, her boredom, she turned to the one gleam of excitement and colour, of possible dream-like escape – the railway that passed along the embankment at the bottom of the garden. Every day there were not only a number of local trains, but several long expresses that thundered by on their way from Cornwall to Bristol and London, and further afield – to Birmingham, to Sheffield, to Liverpool, to Scotland. She could tell the expresses by the whine and thunder of their extra speed. Whenever she heard the familiar noise she ran out into the garden to savour the drama of their passing. To her their gold and brown colours, their streamlined shapes, were a marvellous thing – more marvellous and wonderful than all the surrounding countryside. They were symbols of all that cosmopolitan, colourful world of towns and cities and people which she vaguely remembered from her youth. As each coach rattled past she stared upon it eagerly, as if seeking to devour some taste of its inner world. And when the train was gone, vanished into a puff of smoke, she was not at once forlorn, for some of the glamour remained with her. In her imagination she was aboard it, being carried swiftly into all the wild excitement of a distant world of cities and people, voices and machines. Often she dreamed about this, too, and sometimes the feeling grew upon her so strongly that she could not but believe in her eventual escape, her ultimate freedom from the stolid boredom of her husband, the nervous clinging of his child, the drab, grey, crushing granite of the cottage all round her. Sometimes, indeed she prayed for her deliverance.

One afternoon in autumn, her prayer seemed to be answered. She was in the garden, hanging up some clothes, when her ears caught the puffing of an engine coming down the line. Something in the sound was strange enough to make her pause and look, though she knew it was not one of the expresses. It was, in fact, an engine on its own, a squat, black, grimy engine steaming along slowly; dawdling in fact.

The woman watched its lazy approach with a curious sensation of nervousness. It was as if some thread of contact passed from the engine to herself and back again. The sound of each determined puff of smoke seemed to throb into her body, causing her to tremble. As the engine drew nearer she watched carefully, intently, as if prewarned by some instinct.

To her surprise, the engine now slackened speed and drew to a stop level with the cottage. She saw a lever shut off, heard a hiss of escaping air, and a man, the driver, came and leaned over the rail and called out towards her. She could not properly hear what he said. Slowly she walked down the path until she was quite close to the engine, now looming over her like a great dark bird, and suggesting an impression of power. Suddenly it seemed to darken the sky, to blot out the light of the day. In its shadow she felt afraid, and yet intrigued.

'Hullo there!' called out the engine driver.

76

'Hullo,' said the woman.

She shielded her eyes and stared up at the man leaning over the side rail. He wore oily blue overalls and a peaked railwayman's cap, pulled at a rakish angle over his forehead. He seemed curiously identified with the engine, as if perhaps welded into that throbbing background of pistons and levers, snouts and funnels, hissing steam and glowing red shadows from the open furnace. Behind its caking and grime and sweat she saw that his face was small and sharp featured. The brown eyes shone bright and beady as they darted restlessly from side to side. When his gaze rested upon her she stirred uneasily, yet when he looked away she wanted him to face her, to look back at her. His mouth was fixed in what seemed an easy grin, but she observed the sharpness of the teeth, the tight curl of the lips. There was something almost wolfish in his expression, before which she was fascinated.

'A pretty lonely spot this,' said the driver, wiping a handkerchief across his face.

'Yes,' said the woman. 'Very lonely.'

The driver tipped up his cap and she saw that he had blond, almost golden, hair that contrasted incongruously with the dirt.

'I've often noticed you.' He spoke with care. 'Every time there's a train you come out in the garden to watch, don't you? I know, because I've noticed. Some of my mates have, too.' He looked at her, a sudden pressure behind his gaze before which she wanted to yield, to look away.

'I've wondered more than them, as a matter of fact.'

The woman stared back at him defiantly. 'Have you?'

'Aye.'

His gaze travelled past her, to the pathway, the cottage, to where the child sat watching.

'Your kid?'

'Yes.'

'You're married then?'

'Yes.'

He smiled slowly, but without mirth. 'But still lonely, eh?'

This time she met his gaze look for look, challenge for challenge, boldness for boldness.

'Yes,' she said, and it was a commitment, a declaration of her position.

He leaned forward slightly and she felt – as much as saw – his eyes moving slowly about her being. No man had ever looked at her quite like that before, yet she knew instinctively that she wanted to be looked at in just that way. The knowledge of his eyes upon her was as vivid and startling as a caress. Indeed, in the moment, she trembled, as if some faint caressing touch flickered about her body, touching her breasts and trickling like the flow of gentle water over her shoulders and back and down between her warm thighs. Her mouth went quite dry.

'Well ... ' he said, and she saw his teeth bared, the sharp points pressed together tightly. 'Well, now ...'

He peered up and down the line, then back at his controls, and finally looked at his watch.

'I'm testing out this engine, see? I do a run up to the junction and then back again. But I'm all right for a while. So ...'

He looked at her inquiringly. Then, as if recognising her he gave a little chuckle.

'Well, what are we waiting for, eh?' he said, with superb insolence, and with a swift, lithe movement he jumped out of the cab onto the embankment.

Before his confident approach, the woman stood immobile, her fists clenched, as if in a trance. When he reached her side he touched her elbow gently, and it seemed to break the spell. She was overwhelmed by the enveloping aroma of smoke and grime and sweat and coal dust and fire-fumes; and shining through it all, his foxy, agile presence. She had the impression of the great iron engine's shadow falling all around her. She would not be able to escape its darkness, even if she wished. Without a word she turned and led the way back along the path.

When they came to the doorway he paused.

78

'The child?'

Still without speaking she picked up the little boy, as if he were a bundle of clothes, and carried him quickly into the cottage and up to his cot in a small back room. When he started to cry she gave him a quick slap across his legs. The child was so startled that he subsided into round-eyed silence. She tucked in the blanket and closed the door mechanically, as if she had just performed a service to some stranger. Then she walked to the top of the stairs and looked down to where the engine driver stood with one foot on the first step. She met his gaze in silence, almost stonily, aware instinctively that he knew his purpose. His confidence embraced her, she felt somehow that he would understand all her distorted longings.

The driver took a step forward. He spoke in a whisper. 'Yes, I've wondered. Every time I've seen you I've wondered. If you were alive, really alive ... If you could feel things, if you could do things ...'

He stared at her fixedly and she saw that he was breathing rather heavily, as if controlling himself. The excitement communicated itself, so that her bosom began to rise and fall with the sudden emotion. She felt all her strength leaving her before his will. For she was aware, with a sweet ecstasy she had never before experienced, of this man's implacable intentions. She knew, as she had never known with her husband, that the foxy gaze and sharp teeth would ferret their way to every corner, into every cave of secrecy. And in the knowledge, against which there was no defence, she knew a wonderful liberating sense of fulfilment.

'Oh,' she exclaimed. 'Oh ... Oh ...'

At the sound of her voice he came quickly up the stairs, with the soft, springy steps of a cat, until he stood close beside her. Although she had imagined him as a small man, now he seemed much taller, towering above her.

She felt the last vestige of strength ebbing away. She would have swooned in that moment had he not swiftly bent and taken her in his arms and carried her into the bedroom. She felt him kick the door shut behind, and then he laid her gently upon the thick golden bedquilt. With an instinctive movement she held up her arms towards him, and he bent towards her. She felt his brown eyes piercing into her being, and gave herself up gladly to their gaze.

'I've not felt this before. Never. I've never known … I … ' But she could find no words. He spoke gently to her.

'You've never been alive. I could see that. You've been dead. All the time.'

And then, as she made a vague movement of protest, he grinned and added, 'But it's not your fault. No, it's not been your fault.'

And his hands began running up and down her body skilfully, removing first one article of clothing and then another, while she watched in wonderment through half-closed eyes.

'Not your fault,' he whispered again and again, sometimes close to her ear. 'You're not like that inside, are you? I could see that, too. Ah, my lovely …'

When she was naked he held himself back, appraising her revealed beauty. She lay in an abandoned yet curiously watchful position, and the awareness of it lent added pleasure to his gentle caresses. At each touch of his small, warm hands, the woman felt a tremble ripple through her body, as a wave of the sea – felt her flesh move to meet the embrace.

'Ah!' said the man, 'you're a lovely one, my dear. So white and smooth and warm to the touch.'

And as he spoke, with a sly grin he touched her with an intimate, knowing gesture, watching her eyes as he did so. And perhaps it was the revelation in her eyes, or perhaps the cry forced between her teeth that brought an end to his delicate patience. She was aware of him suddenly looming forward, a huge, inevitable shadow, smelling of oil and grease, smoke and steam, fire and flame, blotting out the light, the room, the world itself.

With a smothered cry she wound her arms fiercely around his slim back, digging her nails deep into his flesh, pulling him frenziedly into that secret, burning place which had existed

barrenly for so many years in her yearning heart. She knew
neither time nor place, only the moment, which lifted her out
of the sloth of emptiness and transported her, as did the
passing express trains, into a rainbow-like, whirling, dazzling
world of dreams.

When he had gone she lay on the bed, incapable of movement.
Turning her head to one side she watched him through the
window, climbing up the embankment and boarding his
black, squat engine. In a moment he had become a part of the
machine again, caught up into a rhythm of levers and handles
and hissing steam. As the engine began to move, with a great
roar and clouds of smoke, she sat up in bed, fearful at the idea
of his departure. She had an impulse to run to the window and
call out, 'Come back, come back!' But she knew he would
never hear her voice against the thunderous blast of his
engine. She lay back in bed, half in ecstasy, half in tears,
thinking about what had been and what might be. And as she
did so her body seemed to leave her. All its sensations were
travelling away down the railway line, seeking the hissing
steam, the pounding wheels, the hard irresistible plunge of the
pistons, penetrating deep into her being. And so, even as she
felt the fear of loss, she knew triumph of possession. Wherever
he went she would secretly be with him, a part of him, of the
oil, the smoke, the reverberating steel monster. And she
smiled at the thought and fell into a deep sleep.

He came again two days later. As soon as she heard the engine
slackening speed, she went to find the child and put him to
bed. When the driver had climbed down the embankment and
started up the pathway, she was standing at the doorway
watching him. She fancied she could smell him across the
distance. The now familiar aroma of his coal-scented sweat
was richer to her nostrils than all the honeysuckle and heather
of the valley. She waited immobile until he came right up to
the door and then, still hardly moving, she allowed the
dressing gown she had slipped on to fall gently to the floor,

leaving her naked before his eyes. It was a simple, perhaps naive, gesture, but the only one she could think of to emphasise to him her complete and utter surrender of herself into his possession.

It was a time of no words. His bright eyes burned upon her flesh. Silently he took her in his arms, covering her face, her neck, her shoulders, her breasts, with his hot savage kisses. When she cried out with pleasure he smiled his mirthless smile, and picked her up and carried her upstairs. In the room where so often she had lain unfulfilled beside her sleeping husband, this man brought her liberation and ecstasy, before which she was humble and his abject slave. It did not then occur to her that he might not feel the same, that he perhaps could not know liberation who had never known imprisonment.

After that, for several weeks, they met frequently. It was a stroke of luck that he had temporarily been put on to testing out a number of local engines, he explained. She did not really take in the implications of his remarks. She did not think at all beyond the almost daily miracle, the dark shadow against the sky-line, the familiar figure on the pathway, the obliteration upon the bed. The time in between hardly existed. Her husband, the child, were shadowy figures, seen through a haze. Vaguely she performed the necessary household duties, cooking their meals, washing their clothes. But at night, in the darkness, when the remote stranger beside her turned with whispering movements, she was harsh and irritable and would not heed his advances. Whatever else she could bear, she felt she could not bear to be touched except by those crafty, life-giving, soul-destroying hands that came to her from the hot furnaces and steel shapes of their daily work.

Now their love-making had softened to allow conversation. And, indeed, the engine driver had a silky voice to which she listened with pleasure, feeling it spinning webs about her as expertly as his hands. He liked talking, too. He talked about life always in terms of his job. In the normal way he drove the express trains which she had so often watched rushing by, and he spoke of them now as a captain might of his ship, recalling the long trips from one end of the country to another. As eagerly he described to her the large towns which his job had taken him to, each place became gay and alive, almost cosmopolitan, filled with bright cafes and glittering pubs, and people, people, people. It began to seem to her that he had friends everywhere, and gradually a fearful jealousy was born in her which she suppressed with difficulty. To comfort herself she indulged in wild fantasies of escape. She played with the quite impossible but fascinating image of him carrying her not into the deathly cottage, but back to the embankment, back to his secretive world, the smoky, hot engine cabin. Sometimes she had strange, erotic dreams where the two of them were surrounded by hissing steam and roaring flames, driving a hurtling ghostly train into eternity. She would not mind, she would mind nothing, if she were with him, within the compass of his caressing hands.

'Oh!' she cried one day, desperately. 'Take me with you! Take me with you!'

'But how can I? It's impossible. I'd lose my job!' he protested.

And before such a prospect she could see clearly that he recoiled – as if (and perhaps it was true) without his familiar environment, his armour of grease and sweat and movement, he would be suddenly bereft and lost, without identity.

'It wouldn't be possible,' he said hastily, but indulgently. And he smiled down at her compensatorily, while his hands fluttered about her body with their deliberate pleasure. 'But don't you bother your head with silly ideas. Don't you bother your head at all, my lovely one. Don't think, just feel ... there, my darling, do you feel? There, there, what else is there in life?'

And, helpless at his touch, she came to believe that, for her, there was indeed nothing else. Yet deep down in her stirred the terrible knowledge that perhaps for him there was something else, some other world beyond her reach.

At first she tried to pretend otherwise, that she did not

possess this awful secret. But the knowledge was always there, locked up irretrievably in her consciousness. It exuded a subtle poison that spread tenuously through her mind, her way of thinking, entering into her very relationship with him.

'Tell me!' she would cry, even in moments of lust, of pleasure, 'tell me you belong to me! Tell me you love me! Tell me, tell me, tell me ...'

But even as he told her, she could not quite believe him. She would listen impatiently, almost irritably. And then when he had finished, when he was exhausted with the mass of verbiage, she would whisper maddeningly. 'Do you really love me? Are you sure? Tell me ...'

After a while of these questions he would fall silent. Fearful, she would burst violently into movement, her hands caressing him urgently, her mouth seeking his, her being spilling over its passions and desires, unsatisfied until he had been caught up in the floodtide, until he had ridden to the point of no return and they were embarked once more upon the uncomplicated process of passion and consummation. Yet at the end of it all, exhausted, some flicker of unease still stirred in her, and she would still whisper, partly to herself. 'Take me away! Take me away!' – until, hearing it, helpless, he turned to one side and fell asleep.

As these fears flickered and glowed within her, she became increasingly alarmed at what might happen. One day when he did not come she paced about the cottage like a person half-demented, kicking at the furniture – and even the child – in her frustration. At night she could not sleep, not for an instant, but stared endlessly out of the window, starting up at the sight of the occasional night train flaming through the darkness. In the morning she looked so haggard and worn that her husband was concerned.

'Leave me alone,' she said irritably. 'I'm all right. I'll be all right.'

And when, about mid-day, the engine came as usual, she was all right. The paleness and the weariness seemed to vanish with the moment. She glowed again with all that unearthly loveliness that his first visit had bestowed upon her. Coming into the cottage uncertainly, he was at once swept up into the sweet savagery of their mutual passion.

But there were other days when he did not come. And gradually he began to drop half-hearted hints that his job might come to an end, that he might have to go away again.

'Back to the expresses, I mean. That's my proper job, you see.' And he grimaced. 'This – this is just a hack sort of job for an experienced driver like me. Now on the expresses ...'

Horrified, she understood how much he belonged not to herself, but to his work, to the engines.

Finally, one day he told her. 'I've been recalled. The job's finished. I'm back on the expresses. Starting tonight. You'll hear me come by, I expect.'

He hesitated, and his foxy face suddenly seemed to her unbearably crafty, cunning beyond comprehension.

'Course, that needn't alter things altogether. I'll have to be away a lot, you'll understand that. But there'll be times ... I'll fix to come over from the junction. I've got a bike, I can ride over.'

Even as he spoke, she knew that he was mouthing words that had no meaning. She did not believe he would come, never again. And even if he did, somehow the idea of him reduced to the ordinary, riding on a bicycle – it was bathos. She could not bear to think of it.

All the same, she could not escape from her fear. 'Don't go! Take me with you!'

And as she pleaded she gave him her lips pressed his hands on her breasts, wound her white legs around him in a frenzy of possession.

'But what can I do?' He looked at her innocently, as if expecting her to understand. 'It's my job, don't you see?'

When the time came for him to go, she became violent in her frenzied protests. She clung to him wildly, stubbornly, even perhaps madly, until he grew afraid.

'I must go. You'll have to let me go. Otherwise there'll be trouble –'

But she obviously did not, could not hear him. He tried to walk out of the cottage and she wound her arms around his waist, pulling him down, trying to drag him out of his life and purpose. In the end, frightened, he struck her, across the face, upon her shoulders, beating at her desperately with his clenched fists until her hold broke and she collapsed moaning upon the floor.

Without looking back, he ran down the path and climbed the embankment. By the time she dragged herself wearily to her feet swift puffs of smoke were shooting up from the engine, and it began moving inexorably along the line. She watched dully until it was a black smudge on the horizon – and then nothing, not even a smudge. And then she sat down at the table and buried her face in her hands.

She was still there when her husband arrived back from work, pushing his bicycle methodically up the path and into the shed. When he came in the doorway and saw her he gave a cry of alarm.

'What is it? Aren't you well? Shall I get a doctor?'

She hardly heard his anxieties. She merely pushed him with one arm, crying out, shouting, telling him to go away. He did not know what to do, he had never had an experience of this sort, but he sensed that she should be left alone. He made his own supper, offering her a little which she refused, and then went out to dig in the garden before it got dark. At sunset he came in again, and moved around restlessly. At last he suggested, nervously, that they should go to bed. By now it seemed to him that she was weak, and that perhaps he could carry her up to bed. But when he bent down to pick her up she twisted in revulsion. For a moment she glared at him. Then, before he could stop her, she hit him across the face, a great blind heave of the hand that sent him half sprawling. An ugly red weal burned across his cheek.

'My God!' he cried out. 'You must be mad.'

And, looking at her in horror, he saw that she was indeed mad, or at least temporarily unbalanced. For her eyes were open and dilated, filled with a fierce, burning brightness

86

before which he flinched and looked away.

'Come to bed,' he pleaded urgently. 'Come and rest. You're – you're – ' What? He did not know. He had no conception. She was a stranger to him. He realised all these things in that moment, as she went out of the door and out of his life.

When he pulled himself together and dashed after her, she was nowhere to be seen. There was no moon that night, only darkness everywhere. He stood irresolute, worried. Then, assuming that she would take the only possible path of escape, the way across the fields to the land and the village, he set off in that direction. It didn't occur to him that there could be another way of escape.

For a long time the woman lay sobbing at the foot of the railway embankment. She was hardly aware that she had left the cottage. She did not really know that her husband had come home. She remembered nothing of his concern, their row, her abrupt departure. She thought only of the afternoon, of her lover, of their parting. 'The job's finished. I'm back on the expresses. Starting tonight. You'll hear me come by, I expect.'

She could hear his voice now, silky and arrogant. She heard it echoing through the night, now soft, now loud. She remembered his lover's phrases, the whispered endearments. 'Now, my lovely one ... there's a lovely one ... I've often wondered if you could feel, if you could do things.' She wanted to swoon again at the thought of his touch, their fusion, their ecstasy. But another voice sounded, strident and cruel, harsh and final. 'The job's finished, the job's finished ...'

Suddenly she screamed out with the pain of it. Her eyes filled with tears of frustration, of helplessness – and finally of hate. Without knowing it she ground her teeth together in a fury of despair. And into the night's wind, she spoke to her lover.

'You belong to me ...'

And as she repeated the words over and over again, they began to assume reality. He belonged to her. He belonged to her. At the thought a half-crazed smile lit up her face, giving it a strange and terrible beauty. Of course! He belonged to her. How foolish of him to think otherwise. How silly of the foxy-face man to think he could escape, to wish to vanish from her life. He belonged to her.

Slowly she pulled herself to her feet, and with infinite patience lifted her weary body up the embankment until she stood on the railway track. In the distance, almost lost in the night air, she heard the faint whistle of a train. The fact registered vaguely on her mind at first, but then with increasing importance. 'You'll hear me come by, I expect ...'

The smile on the woman's face as she turned and began walking along the railway line was one of beautiful ecstasy. She was no longer crazed or maddened with fear, but strangely calm and at peace. She was a woman walking to meet her lover. And as she walked along, treading from one wooden sleeper to another, she seemed to see his sharp foxy face before her, the teeth bared, the bright eyes staring at her, burning with desire, undressing her, caressing her. Soon, soon, out of the night his delicate caressing hands would come, to lift her up gently, to touch her body into excitement, into pleasure, into life.

She heard the whistle again, louder now, and felt the gleaming railway lines trembling beside her. Looking up she saw a faint glow of red outlined in the sky ahead of her. Her heart leaped. He was coming then, coming for her after all! And as the thought in all its triumph and wonder fell upon her, she remembered her lover, she thought swooningly of the implacable obliteration of her personality beneath the power that swept him over her, with which he bent her down and down into unbelievable dark waters of drowning passion. She knew she belonged to him irrevocably.

She walked on down the railway track. She was no longer of her former world, or of any other world. She belonged to the world of her lover, of snorting, primeval, metal monsters. She was caught up in their iron frenzy, their steel passion. She was at one with them, and with her lover. When, at last, she saw him racing to meet her – the shining teeth, the flaming snout, the familiar, all-embracing aroma of flame and soot, smoke and devouring flame – she cried out his name in blind, oblivious ecstasy. And gladly, she ran forward to meet his last, terrible embrace.

Two days later he read of the accident in the newspaper. He was horrified and tried to figure out the time. Could it have been? Was it possible? He could not be sure. Wisely, he did not try to find out.

III

This Old House

I first saw the old house in Tregorran Valley when I was a small boy. It had been planted firmly among the gentle folds of the surrounding moors and from the back it seemed to be perpetually in shadow. But the massive front porchway looked out over a winding, tangled footpath that led down to a sandy cove and white-crested Atlantic rollers and all sorts of mystery beyond.

It was the sort of deserted house you read about in romantic novels. I suppose it was because of this atmosphere that it held such a fascination for my father. He was a writer of books himself and it was upon his continual ability to imagine all sorts of fanciful plots that he and my mother and I depended for our daily bread and the comfort of a small cottage high up on the moors – where I might say we were exposed not only to the wildness of the elements, but even more to relentless pressures from a variety of creditors.

At such times my father invariably fled, leaving my poor mother to fight an uneasy rearguard action ... and invariably, often with myself as companion, he would seek asylum in the old house in the valley. There he would wander around the many rooms in a sort of ecstasy – indeed, it soon became quite obvious to me that already my father looked on this vast empty building as his own property.

It was a sad irony that just at this time our family fortunes seemed to plunge to their lowest ebb. My father worked hard enough indeed; often I would start up in the night to hear the familiar clicking sound of his typewriter. Almost every day my mother or I would walk over to the village to post off a manuscript; but a few days later it always seemed to come back again.

It must have been very worrying even for my father, but somehow he always seemed to have a kind of bottomless resilience to fall back on, there was always another manuscript, another tomorrow.

But somehow, this time, my mother grew more and more depressed. She began to mope about the house in a way quite despairing, even for her – as if she was beginning to give up hope not just for the moment, but forever.

One morning there was a particularly depressing post. After we had read the letters my mother sat in silence, fingering through the envelopes forlornly as if hoping against hope to find some consolation. All at once she screwed up her face and then burst into a terrible bout of weeping, burying her head in her hands and sobbing away.

'It's no good,' she sobbed. 'We can't go on … we'll never be able to manage … it's the end of everything.'

I looked nervously at my father, wondering uneasily if he was about to make his usual escape. But this time he did not. He watched with seeming impassivity for a few moments, then he leaned across the table and touched my mother gently on the shoulder.

'Don't cry, sweetheart.' For a moment, I think, he hesitated; and then, almost blurting out the offer, he said:

'Look, I tell you what – you come along with us. I've got – I've got something I want to show you.'

I looked at my father in surprise. I half rose in readiness to accompany them, but my father gave me a quick look of warning, and I realised that this time I was not needed. A few moments later full of sudden brisk good spirits, my father was ushering my mother off with him towards the moors.

After a while my curiosity got the better of me, and I went after them. I took good care to keep well out of sight but I hardly need have bothered. My father's whole attention seemed to be given up to his companion, as if in some way he was doing his best to persuade her out of that mood of despondency. From afar at last I heard the rusty creak of the gates and I fancied I heard my mother's voice raised in protest. She was a great stickler for the correct procedure and I could well imagine her demurring at any intrusion on private property. I could also imagine the grandiloquent gestures with which my father would throw open the gates and beckon my mother up the drive.

When finally I reached the front of the house there was no sign of either of them, but the front door was ajar. I tip-toed up the steps and into the hallway. I could hear the echo of footsteps upstairs, and then voices, suddenly becoming louder. Quickly I went over to a small alcove and pressed myself back against the wall well out of sight.

I was only just in time, for a moment later I heard my mother and father coming down the wide sweeping staircase. I peeped round and saw that my father had his arm round my mother's shoulders in a curiously protective way, and I imagined perhaps she had been crying.

When they reached the bottom of the stairs my mother looked around rather sadly, as if to say, 'Well, yes, but what's the point of –'

And then, just as indeed my mother was opening her mouth to say something no doubt eminently practical, my father suddenly seemed to come vividly to life. It was as if suddenly the spell was working, and all at once he had entered into the dream world where this old house was really his old house. As I watched he turned and bowed extravagantly low to my mother, as if welcoming her to her manorial home.

It seemed to me that my mother half raised her hand as if in vague protest. Then I heard the sound of my father's laughter and with a movement of complete naturalness he took my mother's arm and, very gravely, began to waltz her round the hall. It was a big hallway and they were at the far end so I could not hear what my mother said, but I could imagine her instinctively protesting.

But the funny thing was that by the time they had waltzed their way over to my corner my mother didn't seem to be protesting any longer. I caught a glimpse of her as she whirled by in my father's arms and she had her eyes closed and her face lifted up and it seemed to me that her lips were touched by a gentle, rather sweet smile – as if, why, as if in some quite unexpected way she was actually enjoying this madcap moment – as if somehow, miraculously, my father's dreams had become reality.

Round and round they waltzed, pirouette after pirouette ... and as their slow, graceful movements whirled before my eyes it was not at all difficult for me to imagine the years and years falling away; this old house a living thing again, the floors polished, the walls draped, the fire blazing, the chandelier glittering as it swung slowly round, everywhere the bright colours of the ladies' gowns and the men's uniforms; the air full of laughter and life ...

When at last my mother and father stopped dancing round the light was beginning to fade. I saw them exchange a long glance, and then my father smiled, rather youthfully, and put an arm round my mother, and together they went slowly out of the front door on their way home. I waited a few minutes to give them time to return home, and then I set off slowly along the path after them. Somehow I was in no hurry to reach home. I knew that when I went in my father might well be reading his newspaper again and my mother busy with her ironing or something ... and perhaps that was as it should be. But for myself I held a sweet little secret deep in my youthful heart: and nothing about my parents would ever again be ordinary or dull or mundane – but always a marvel and a wonder.

IV

The Maid

Every morning around ten o'clock the young Irish girl in the neat black and white maid's uniform began her routine tour of the fifth-floor bedrooms of the large old-fashioned hotel. She had been told by the older woman who first took her round always to rattle her keys noisily as she came down the corridor and always to knock loudly three times before attempting to enter ... but she had found from experience that by such a late hour all the guests were usually up and away ... and so perhaps as she daydreamed her way through the boring procedures thinking about Lough Rae and her little home near Roosky on the distant Shannon she had grown a trifle casual in the manner of her approach.

One morning she knocked perfunctorily at the door of the tenth bedroom along, turned her master key in the lock and opened the door wide – to find standing in the middle of the room the white and naked body of a young man. In the frozen cinematic moment that followed, the girl's bright startled eyes seemed to absorb every little detail of the scene so that it was forever afterwards etched into her memory – the body taut and supple and strangely beautiful, leaning forward a little so that the head and shoulders were hunched up powerfully like a boxer's; the neck, curiously graceful, now turned swiftly in her direction so that she could not avoid meeting a gaze as startled as her own yet somehow (she remembered later) by no means over-embarrassed; the face of a man, hardly that, a boy of her own age, a neatly formed face with very high cheekbones and unusually fair eyebrows and above a mop of curly fair hair.

'Oh!' exclaimed the girl, as startled as if it had been herself so dramatically disturbed.

If the young man had turned away, had fled or even collapsed in total confusion and shame, possibly the girl might have managed to withdraw with at least some of her composure preserved. But in fact, mysteriously, bafflingly, the young man remained unmoved, carved as if into a stone statue, with just the faintest of smiles touching his soft fresh lips. And so fatefully despite all the externally imposed modesty of her conventional upbringing the girl was unable to stop the almost sensual journey of her eyes downwards, tracing with strange and unfamiliar delight the tapering lines of the youthful body, down and down to the sudden swell of thigh and muscle and the stark and unmistakable symbol of manhood.

'Oh, sorry – excuse me, I'm sure,' said the girl hastily, in a jumble of distorted sound. And this time, as if breaking some spell, she wheeled round and almost ran out of the room, slamming the door behind her. Yet even as she did so she was left with the haunting sensation of the young man still unmoved, his face still wearing that almost amused expression, his soft brown eyes following her out of the room and down the long long corridor and forever into the life ahead.

For some time the girl could not bring herself to mention the experience to any of her workmates. By a great effort of will she forced herself to go on with her morning's tasks though by now rattling her keys endlessly and knocking not once but four or five times at each door. When that work was finished she went into the small canteens where the girls prepared morning cups of coffee and helped herself to a much needed black coffee. She noticed that her hand was still trembling from the recent shock as she raised the cup to her lips. So did one of the other women who asked if she was feeling all right. Yes, the girl said, she was feeling fine ... but in reality she was feeling somehow as she had never felt before in her life: a mixture of fear and excitement, of pain and pleasure, of perplexity and revelation. And, she had to confess, hardly a glimmer of shame.

After a while the girl found this confusion of sensations too much to bear and so, later in the day, she confessed to one of the elder women something (but not all) of what had happened.

The other woman, with her matter of fact reception of the news, brought a momentary relief.

'Goodness, love, that's nothing – you should see some of the sights I've had the bad luck to see!'

After that it was possible, at least publicly, to turn the whole episode into some kind of joke, like something out of a magazine or told by a friend. Values were coarsened, truth reduced, accuracy blunted and a way of bearing the shock was available.

The disturbing thing was, the girl found that evening when her duty was over and she sat in her tiny attic bedroom high up in the hotel, that privately she did not want to take advantage of the escape. Privately, deep down in her secret self, she wanted to savour, to remember, even to relive the whole process of events ... and even if the wish had not been a conscious one she knew that, subconsciously, she could never have freed herself from the repetitive and vivid images that now came swirling around her: images that were white and precise and young and fresh and beautiful, and always of a smiling young man with sandy hair and an untouched and virginal body.

That night the young Irish girl, far from the safe channels of her home land, was almost afraid to go to sleep for fear of what dreams might come. In fact sleep was loth to come at all and for hour after hour she lay tense and uneasy in her narrow bed, staring dry-eyed and apprehensive through the fearful darkness.

When it was time the next morning for the young girl to unlock the tenth bedroom door she felt herself overcome by nervousness: her brow was flushed, her hands trembled, her throat was suddenly parched. She stood irresolute in the middle of the corridor eyeing the closed door in front of her and it was as if her feet were mysteriously chained to the floor.

Then at last perhaps some spark of Irish bravado entered into the girl's soul and with an almost superhuman effort of will she advanced, rattling her keys agitatedly before finally unlocking the door. When she swung it open and advanced in she had the almost hallucinatory sensation of having stepped out of time: this was not new but another time, it was yesterday, *the* yesterday ... But when she opened her eyes, that had closed involuntarily, she found herself staring around an empty and suddenly desolate room.

It was tantalising to the girl that the moment she discovered the room to be empty she found herself secretly wishing that this was not so – that, indeed, it was still yesterday. This thought, with its peculiar and almost lewd undertones, gave her an enormous illicit sort of pleasure: for several moments she walked about with her eyes closed, imagining it was not the shadowy present but the vivid past.

Then, opening her eyes more practically, she began looking round the room for some tangible echoes of the missing young man. Her first fearful thought was that he might have gone but this was allayed by the sight of a green sweater thrown carelessly over the back of a chair. She went over and picked this up, feeling the thick wool thoughtfully, finally raising it and rubbing the rough texture against her cheek. The touch was harsh and unfamiliar to her soft skin, painful rather than pleasurable, and yet she kept up the rubbing movement, almost perversely.

After a while the girl put down the sweater and began moving about the room, opening cupboards and wardrobes and drawers – it was something, she knew, which she was strictly supposed not to do but somehow she found she could hardly help herself. She felt possessed by an imperious desire to know something about this stranger, to be able to formulate at least some coherent background to all the knowledge she had, which remained misty and erotic. At first she was disappointed: coat, trousers, shirt, socks, shoes – they all seemed curiously anonymous, leaving her mind still blank. Then, idly opening a suitcase at the foot of the bed the girl's attention was suddenly riveted as she saw a large and beautifully printed folder, the cover dominated by a striking photograph of a nude girl. Inside, the book was lavishly illustrated with more nude photographs – all rather exotic and lovely, yet all somehow unreal and dead.

The girl stood looking down at these beautiful dead women in confusion, aware of a sense of rivalry and even jealousy – and then, almost without being conscious of the action, she began slowly running her hands over the shape of her own body, feeling its pulsating reality, its warm flesh and blood, its life. All at once she smiled secretively to herself, knowing even in her youthful innocence that any young man who kept folders of nude photographs was very much a lonely and unfulfilled young man. And so ...

Still with that secret smile playing at her lips the young girl began cleaning and tidying the room, performing each gesture with some kind of special significance. She would, as yet, have felt startled and embarrassed if the young man had returned suddenly: she had not yet assimilated enough of his personality to be able to feel at ease with him. Indeed, once or twice, hearing movements in the corridor she froze into immobility, her heart beating rapidly, her face suffused with colour. But when the movements had passed she calmed down and forced herself not to panic, to continue with her exploration not so much of a mere room as of a mysterious fellow human being.

When at last the girl let herself out of the room and walked away down the corridor she felt a curious sense of new intimacy with the unknown young man, a composite of the photographs of the nude girls and the image of the young man's own nakedness, of the roughness of his green sweater and the remembered smoothness of his smile. Bearing this strange portrait with her she walked along, smiling secretively and softly – and somehow never noticed the young man as he came up the stairs and stood abruptly to one side, watching her as she passed with a mixture of curiosity and wonderment. When finally she had disappeared from sight the young man hurried to his room and went in and stood looking almost angrily at the folder of photographs, finally throwing it away disconsolately into the suitcase.

After that near encounter the movements of the girl and the young man became like threads in a pattern, weaving some mysterious warp. One morning she saw him emerge from his room abruptly, like a flash of golden sunlight, and unable to stop herself she darted into a doorway and stood watching from a distance as he strode away – when she went into his room a few moments later it was still warmly permeated with his presence, the odour of his body borne like a feather on a breeze, and strangely sweet to her nostrils. One afternoon the young man, turning a corner suddenly, saw the girl helping to unload a trolley piled high with bedclothes – each time she stretched up to lift down the next bundle he was hypnotised by her supple movements, the rustle of the stiff clothes on the unseen flesh inside seemed to protest against such barbarous imprisonment. And one evening, though each was unaware of the fact, they were alone in a long street and walking towards one another when some strange impulse prompted each in turn to alter course, the man to go back for something he had forgotten, the girl to cross the road to look in a shop window.

And now all the time the girl found herself thinking not so much about the young man as about the whole of her life prospect. It was as if suddenly she had realised there were no more variegated problems or barriers – only the single if perhaps surmountable barrier. At night she sometimes stood in her little bedroom staring at herself in the mirror, slowly taking off her clothes until she had nothing on, and then examining critically the pale limbs thus exposed. Am I pretty?

100

she wondered. Is my body beautiful? And then always –
would *he* think so?

Each new morning that dawned the young girl vowed to
herself: today I must take some action. And so, did she but
know it, did the young man. Yet somehow the right moment
remained elusive and unattained. And all the time, secretly,
the girl worried. Suppose he should leave? And all the time,
did she but know it, the young man worried similarly – for
indeed he was due to leave shortly to take up work in another
town.

Until almost the last day before the young man was due to
leave, when what can only be called a kind of Fate took charge
of events. From a room that was not the young man's at all but
belonged to some bored wealthy old lady a fat finger pressed a
button to summon the maid for some menial task ... only by
some strange chance, an electrical fault, the wrong number
was illuminated in the maid's room so that she set out, a little
nervously, for Room 10.

It is not straining the bounds of credulity too much to assert
that on this particular spring-like morning, for the second
time within a week, the young Irish maid rattled her keys and
turned the lock of Room 10 and went in – and found standing
in the middle of the room the white and naked body of a young
man. The fact was that impelled by some strange erotic fancy,
he had stood naked each morning at that time in the obsessive
desire that the young girl should come in just as she had done
once before. He had no clear idea of the subterranean
impulses that prompted him, what secret hunger – he knew
only that, as if obeying some ancient tribal feeling, he could
only stand there, aware of himself, waiting with a mixture of
hope and despair ...

But this time, as he was delightfully to find out, was to be
very different. For now, as the girl entered, it seemed to her as
if the occasion, apparently the same, was not so at all. This
young god standing before her, naked and unashamed, was no
longer some strange young man – but a human being known
to her secretly and intimately, someone whose darkest and

most primeval thoughts were known and shared by her. This was another human being, a man, towards whom for the first time in her life the girl felt no fear, no apprehension, only a strange and overwhelming tenderness.

The girl came into the centre of the room: behind her the door closed firmly and irrevocably. The young man watched her wonderingly, still transfixed to the spot, his body arched and poised as if for some eternal flight to another world.

As if mesmerised the girl came right up to the young man until she was so near that she could actually feel the heat of his body, smell the perfume of his breath. Then, as if to delay a moment longer might break not only the spell of that moment but perhaps the whole unfolding and beautiful pattern of life itself, the girl began unfastening her blouse and then loosening her clothes.

A moment later, laughing secretly and singing in their hearts, they were clasped together again in that first marvellous embrace of Adam and Eve, of all the world's lovers.

V

Behind The Mask

'Aha!' he said, largely to himself.

He stood before the half open windows of the bedroom looking down upon the curving yellow drive that linked the hotel's refined seclusion with the distant grey rooftops of Falmouth and a fleeting glimpse of the sea. He had cultivated the habit of coming there almost every day, just before lunchtime. It was the most likely period for the day's excitements if there were to be any. People coming and people going, falsely hearty welcomes, unconvincingly sad farewells – sometimes perhaps an extra tit-bit like the arrival of a coach party, all bustle and talk and ladies wearing large floral hats.

He did not like to miss anything, not the smallest scrap of potential human drama. He was always there, hands plunged deep into the bulging pockets of his tweed jacket, bony old body rocking gently backwards and forwards, small inquisitive eyes darting up and down the drive, peering into each corner and cranny of the long rectangular green and granite entrance yard.

'Aha!' he exclaimed again. 'We have visitors, I see.'

And eagerly he focussed his eyes on the familiar blue station taxi as it swept grandly up to the stone pillared porch.

'What's that you say?' murmured his wife. She was lying stretched out on the bed, a grey-haired stoutish woman, her eyes now closed, looking rather pale from one of her frequent head-aches. She turned her head sideways, and frowned at a sudden spasm of pain.

'Would you mind – the aspirins and a glass of water –

would you pass them, dear?' she asked.

'Yes ... yes.' He nodded, still staring out of the window, peering forward to catch the out-flux of people and luggage. 'One moment – just one moment.'

His eyes flickered, rapier-like, from person to person noting colour and contour and width and breadth, even poking under a momentary sun-shadow to catch the mode of the short walk forward that took the actors into the hotel and out of his gaze. Already, confidently, he could piece the jig-saw into its beginning – station-taxi meaning railway journey (almost inevitably from London); small amount of luggage meaning short stay; quality of clothes meaning middle-class; external behaviour of occupants suggesting married couple ...

'Please – the aspirins!'

'Certainly. Of course. The aspirins!' He broke away from the window; useless staring at an empty yard, anyway; moved over to a small medicine cupboard. He found the little white bottle and filled a small tumbler in the adjoining bathroom.

He came over to the bed and handed them, officiously, to the woman on the bed, but without looking directly at her.

'Dear, dear!' he said, tut-tuttingly. 'Very dull visitors, I fear. Not at all what we might call exciting, or even interesting. Mr and Mrs – what shall we say – Smith? Johnson? – possibly, yes, possibly – or a degree better? Perhaps – yes, perhaps, Rodgers. Or thereabouts. Mmhh ... Yes ... Mr and Mrs Rodgers. A rather *ordinary* couple. And somewhat sober in appearance ... They will have a neat, fairly unobtrusive table ... And no doubt keep largely to themselves ... Mmmmh.'

His wife put the bottle carefully on the bed table, the half-emptied tumbler beside. She dipped her fingers in the water and ran their tips gently over her face, bringing a momentary breath of new life as she waited, a little wearily, for the sedative to give its temporary relief.

'Pity,' he went on. 'Great pity.' He sat on the bed, feeling rather let down. No smart, beautiful woman – not even an odd character – to be quizzical about. He sighed, knowing there

was nothing now but to wait for the lunch-gong.
'Headache gone?' he inquired, in a flat voice.

In his seventieth year (and he looked it) Carlton Smithers still
found hotel life possessed of the same irresistible fascination
that had captured him forty years back, when he was just
beginning the brilliant career that had established him as one
of the world's best-known, also best-selling novelists. It was
not so much the hotels themselves, however spacious, however
luxuriously fitted, beautifully situated, efficiently organised –
though these things counted, of course. It was rather the
existence, within a convenient space, of a world of constantly
changing human beings; a world that could be viewed at ease,
attending ritual meals in large comfortable dining-rooms,
strolling about sun terraces and neat-mown lawns, or
conveniently placed in a well-chosen seat in the lounge. He
enjoyed, in particular, the afternoon siestas in long soft-
coloured lounges, with the familiar background; the deep
comfort of the usual corner-armchair, the handy, solid pile of
illustrated magazines, the aroma of black coffee waiting on a
silver tray that was already half-shrouded by the smoke of his
cigar – across the way the equally familiar sight of his wife
dozing off, her square grey head drooping sideways into the
shadow of the winged corner.

From this vantage position he himself appeared as an
arresting, if slightly repulsive, figure; the big stooping frame
twisted up in the rigid mannerism of old age, stoutness
protruding unmistakably under its uneasy covering of full-
blown tweeds. The faint yellow finger of decay had stained its
trail over his face – under hollowing eyes, at the drop of red-
veined cheeks, around the corner of the once-precise mouth,
now loosening and turning down with tiredness. Even so,
much of the tell-tale yellow was overshadowed by the massive
forehead, by the huge, naked gleaming head that ballooned
out in greater proportions than the rest of him, so that it
seemed to rock somewhat precariously upon its narrow neck
stem. It was a powerful and impressive, but also rather

frightening head: impressive and frightening for the same reason, because its beholders could seldom forget that encased within it was that savage, brilliant element, the mind of Carlton Smithers – the mind that could so ruthlessly pierce, dissect, expose and satirise the human frailties of mankind.

When he was a young, not yet quite successful writer – though already a very successful and highly paid partner in a London law practice – he set resolutely about attaining his technical accomplishment. In those days he used to take with him, wherever he went, a thick red notebook. At some time or other – travelling on a bus, walking along a street, sitting in the court – out would come the book and he would painstakingly note down, in his neat hand-writing, the appropriate epithet, the flashing ironic detail, the captured delicate situation. Every night, when he returned home, he sat down and entered into the same business-like notebook any useful points from the evening's conversations, any witty remarks (they were already mostly his own), or idiosyncrasies of speech or behaviour on the part of his host or hostess, of other guests, perhaps a waiter. (Waiters, hotel porters, managers – mostly they had come to irritate him, as they hovered on the outskirts of his life; but he had, from time to time, taken care to note necessary details, as they waited on him, carried his bags, hovered obsequiously around him during each one's ordained duty period.)

In this way, year by year, he had accumulated his vast knowledge of infinite details, so that he could describe comprehensively the way women dressed, the geography of a remote country, the various methods by which men would get drunk, the interior of motor cars of almost any nationality, the sort of jewellery that a Continental ex-princess might wear, the means by which astute American business men amassed their fortunes. With diligent practice he became an adept at the bright venomous record of the hundred and one stupidities and oddities of human behaviour – woman with woman, man with man, above all man with woman. He approached human relationships with the same detached, penetrating mind for

106

detail, noting the familiar gestures, patterns, reactions and moods. And to be sure that he was being thoroughly efficient he carried his investigations into the personal as well as the public arena, embarking on a wide variety of personal relationships, all of which yielded invaluable data.

After all the years of glittering achievement he remained proud of his knowledge and worldliness, the quick, shrewd, wickedly clever judgments he could always make – the fact that, from the depths of his watchful armchair, he could build a frame around the head and shoulders of some distant hotel guest and with a few rapid slashing strokes create the naked, terrible true portrait that lurked under the mask. For, of course, everyone wore a mask: that was apparent to any rational detached observer. It was what lay under the mask that mattered, titillating the writer's imagination, inviting macabre exploration. Under each mask there must inevitably be hidden something fascinating, rather morbid, something delicately indiscreet – preferably something dark and rather dreadful. (Sometimes, of course there was really nothing at all.) To probe down, tear away the puny protective films, plunge straight to the naked nerve centres – that was Carlton Smithers' self-chosen task.

Over the years he had accomplished it brilliantly, not once, but ten, twenty, thirty, forty times; the results could be seen in a score of novels, a dozen plays, a handful of bizarre short stories. It was perhaps natural that after all that time – forty years' inhabitation of thick-carpeted hotel halls, dining-rooms, sun terraces, coffee-lounges – forty years of dressing up for dinner-parties and bridge matches and bright smiling cocktails in modernistic hotel saloons – the mysteries of life appeared conventionally obvious. His mind performed smoothly and automatically, lubricated with the long years' facility, slotting together each jig-saw puzzle with confident, unerring movements – yet it was still with a connoisseur's sensual pleasure that he allowed his cool, dissective eyes to journey from odd-assorted group to strange-paired couple, from red, sweaty face to pale unhappy face, from naive young to weary old, ever finding satisfaction in his swift evaluation of their monotonous, predictable emptiness ...

'I see I was right,' he said, rather pleased with himself, taking the first puff at his cigar after luncheon. 'Our friends, the new arrivals, settled down at the tables by the annexe, for luncheon. Now, they are rather daringly going to have coffee in the lounge. I should say –'

'Yes, dear?' His wife nodded politely, sipping delicately at the coffee. Coffee was one of her greatest delights; she always savoured it to the full. Sometimes it puzzled her to realise how automatically Carlton drank *his* coffee – for, in that case, he obviously derived no true pleasure from it.

'I should say – ' he went on, bending a little forward so that he could get a clearer view between two palm trees, 'I should say that they normally drink water only at lunch. They are not accustomed to the stimulant of coffee afterwards – see how the woman is fidgeting, uneasily, feeling out of place. And the man! Ah, there, my dear, we have a very interesting case. There we have an example of the backbone of the great British race – the unmistakably *little* man.'

He cleared his throat for action.

'Observe. Medium size, stockily built but not overpowerful, neatly cut and parted hair, going a little grey at the sides – from here, of course, I cannot tell, but it is highly likely, highly likely indeed, that the gentleman's suit, though of reasonable quality, has seen ample wear. You see, my dear, this little man that I am talking about, he does not like extravagance. He likes to get his full value out of articles, such as clothing.

'Hum-Hum-Yes,' he decided, aloud, capturing a satisfying phrase. 'Have we not, indeed, an excellent symbol in the suit? Our little man is like his suit – of medium quality, giving medium wear. So much, no more. Rather sad, really, but there it is ... Eh?'

'Yes, dear,' said his wife placidly, while her thoughts darted away on an illicit inspection of her immediate prospects and tasks. The room – yes, she had cleared away those odd, annoying things that were always left lying about by Carlton, making the room seem so untidy. Tea – yes, she had confirmed with the maid that she was to take tea up to Carlton at 4.30, when he would, by routine, be writing in the seclusion of his private study. Herself – yes, she had arranged to meet Mrs Hemmings for a cup of tea and a talk. Such an interesting, brave woman, Mrs Hemmings, running that occupational school for cripples. She was looking forward to giving Mrs Hemmings some much needed help; at least three afternoons a week. Carlton didn't like her to go out too much, but she thought she could manage that, though, of course, it wouldn't be wise to tell him exactly where she was going.

'You agree, then?' he said, nodding his great head inquiringly in her direction.

'Oh ... Yes – yes, dear,' she said a little breathlessly, hoisting her thoughts back abruptly. She knew Carlton expected her always to confirm his opinions. Who had be been referring to? – the people that came just before lunch – somewhere in the far corner, perhaps? Vaguely she saw two unfamiliar silhouettes, sitting close together and talking to each other rather animatedly. She liked new residents. A breath of fresh air, a break in the pattern of familiar faces.

'Now, observe the woman,' he went on, running a long curved finger down the side of his straight, protruding nose – a favourite habit that she could remember from schooldays, when they were neighbouring children.

'The woman – she is more introspective, more emotional – of course, women always are ... Probably she is really the shrewder of the two – yet, on the other side, we must expect that she is far more uneasy, her nerves tensed up much more than his. For she is more the creature of habit, of behaviour pattern, and so it follows ... '

– And it was funny, too, but he had retained not only that but most of his habits. Indeed, she supposed if she tried to count them on her fingers, she would have a poor total of the changes she had seen in him. It was a good thing she had been in love with him. How dreadful to have been married to him otherwise! She gave a faint, hidden smile at the thought. As it was, the love softened the edge of so many wounds, that would otherwise have hurt. It had not been easy, altering herself to fit into his pattern, being always his bright, charming companion, quick to appreciate his quips, his bursts of rude humour ... It had not been easy, these forty-odd years.

'True, she is dressed rather more smartly than the man – that I partly observed on their arrival. But, then, women's entire interest in life is focused on clothes and appearance – er – next to the opposite sex, of course – at least, so I trust?' He cocked a quizzical, pleased eye, partly at his wife, partly around him in case there were any listeners. Unconsciously he had raised his voice.

'Ssssh! You're speaking too loudly, dear,' said his wife suddenly.

'Um? Er – well, all right, all right.' He controlled the errant voice, temporarily.

'As I was saying. Women take care of their appearance and so forth. Hum ... Yes.' It was damnable. The interruption had cut across his train of thoughts, his weaving of threads. He put the cigar down, gulped the remainder of the coffee, picked up the cigar again and took an angry puff, and another, and another. He smokes too much, thought his wife rather sadly; and the funny thing is I don't think he really enjoys it.

'Well – ' He waved an expressive hand. 'There you have them, the typical, humdrum British people.'

He always refers to the British, she thought, as if they were some rather inferior foreign race. It was true, of course, that he had travelled a lot, had been on five cruises round the world. But the fact was he had been born in Leeds and his father had built up his large fortune from the profits of a large textile factory he had been fortunate enough to acquire in a business deal. Thanks to that money, there had been no local school, no humdrum provincial life, no financial or career worries, for Carlton – instead, public school, the University, a nice fat legal practice and an unlimited allowance until the days when his sardonic observations and commentaries on fellow human

110

beings – including, as one of the earliest, a most merciless study of his own family – began paying dividends of fantastic proportions in the form of publishers' royalties.

'I think I'll go to sleep now, dear,' she said hastily, seeing that Carlton was about to continue his narrative.

He frowned across as she smiled apologetically and closed her eyes.

'Very well, very well,' he said. He scanned the room, restlessly, suddenly bored.

'Isn't it time for you to go and do your writing?' murmured his wife from behind the darkening cover of sleepy eye-lids.

'Yes,' he said, seizing on the idea decisively. 'Time for the writing.'

He got to his feet slowly, stretched his long frame, straightened the ruffled waist-coat and brushed some dust off the lapel of his coat. Threading a leisurely yet purposeful way across the lounge he began deliberating upon what he would write, seizing a phrase that had occurred to him, tossing it about and enlarging it into the shape of a possible story. As he neared the big glass doorways he glimpsed a clever, ironic finality. He went out with his great bald head thrown back and a thin, wide smile splitting his face.

At dinner that evening the thick crimson curtains were drawn over and the hall delicately infused with discreetly placed lights, mostly tinged a faint pink. The women had donned shimmery evening dresses and the men, though no longer compelled by convention into full evening-dress, mostly wore dark lounge suits (if they did not, in fact, retain the evening dress custom). A small space in the centre was cleared of tables to permit a certain amount of genteel dancing to the music of a three-piece orchestra. But both the dancing and the music were spread over a long evening, and were somewhat desultory.

'Did you have a good afternoon's work, dear?' she said, as they nibbled some biscuits and cheese. He looks quite pleased, she thought.

'Yes ... Yes, quite a good afternoon,' he admitted. 'And you?' he inquired vaguely, still thinking of his work.

'Oh, a pleasant little outing,' she said calmly. She had met Mrs Hemmings and arranged to go and help her several afternoons a week. They had had such a good heart-to-heart talk. She had come back feeling quite a different woman to the one who went out. She was aware of contentment, knowing of the new purpose and the good it would do.

'Good,' he said, dismissing the perfunctory politeness from his mind now it had been laboriously fulfilled.

'I,' he went on, resuming his original intention, 'I have embarked on a new story. Or perhaps I should call it a study, an analytical study.'

He began rolling a small piece of bread round and round between his forefinger and the table, until the dough squashed into grey putty and became unformed and lifeless.

The three-piece band concluded its fore-gathering, and at a nod of the head from its grey-haired leader began playing a waltz.

'It is my task,' he went on heavily, 'to expose the appalling superficialities and artificialities with which our lives are surrounded. Mmmh ... Yes. Indeed, one might well say such is my mission as a writer.'

'Yes, dear, you have worked very hard,' said his wife, turning her eyes sideways so that she could watch the dancing. She noted with amusement the old General gallantly partnering his rather clumsy wife. Neither of them could be said to dance properly but every evening they took the floor three or four times, and they seemed to enjoy the fun of it.

'Perhaps you may remember, in the third of my series of autobiographical books, there is a passage, beginning of chapter four – no, no, chapter five –' He paused sidetracked for a moment into a memory chase through the 300-odd pages of the book. He recollected how it had been written some ten years previously, while on a yachting cruise in the Mediterranean. He had been a little doubtful about that cruise, but in fact it had been well worth while. Not only had he completed the book he intended to write, but from the variety of complex human beings he had been able to observe within the closely confined quarters of a boat at sea, there had emerged the material for a first-class popular play. It was running in London even now.

'I remember, dear,' nodded his wife.

'Do you?' He shot her a suspicious look. 'Well, in that case I won't recapitulate it all. The essence is – scratch beneath the surface of a human being and you will find, surprisingly quickly, the hollow bones of space.

'Great, thick, unpliable bones of space,' he repeated, with some relish, deriving a peculiar pleasure at the vision of herds of ordinary people composed of millions and millions of hollow bones that crackled and crinkled as he smashed them down with the butt of his walking-stick.

At that moment the band struck up for the third dance. Nearly a dozen couples took the floor, including the new guests. The woman wore a fresh-looking blue organdie dress, the man the same suit as at lunch time. They danced easily and smoothly together.

'There!' exclaimed Carlton Smithers triumphantly, jabbing a lean, arthritical finger towards the dance-floor. 'That is what I mean – the human species gyrating around a small area of polished woodwork, vaguely imitating the animal gestures of their predecessors.' It was a good, striking sentence but his wife had read it before in several of his books, and its effect was largely wasted on her.

'But, Carlton – you used to dance yourself,' she protested. Now he never did, but she hoped that during the evening the General or perhaps Mr Brailsford might come and ask her for the pleasure.

He frowned slightly. He had indeed danced at one time – but that was in the days when he obtained a thrill from the feel of warm and soft female bodies within his arms. Recently, alas, he had discovered the loss of certain of these former exquisite sensations, and to drag around a dance floor became a waste of his time; consequently he did not waste it.

'To proceed,' he said sharply, 'most of the dancers, I fear, are already only too familiar to us.' He stared coldly from one to another, seeing their characters as he had often, malevolently portrayed them in books and stories – emphasising their outstanding and, so far as he was concerned, only relevant features: the drunken general, the twittering dowager, the dull insurance manager, the powdered and painted amateur prostitute of a widow, the shiny-faced Jewish financier and his cunning and voluptuous wife, the pompous white-moustached local MP, the simpering old maiden sisters – Oh, yes, they were spreadeagled like dried butterflies before the eyes of Carlton Smithers, the eye that could strip the false coat of colour and reveal the true drab-dreary skeleton.

Feeling a solid pride, he continued:

'We won't bother with the known. Let us take the unknown – or, hum – hah, I should say, the less known. I refer, of course, to our visitors, the text-book Mr and Mrs Rodgers.'

'Why, of course!' broke in his wife, her face lighting up at a thought remembered. 'I knew I had something to tell you. They were on the bus coming back – they'd been for a walk into Falmouth and bussed back.' She paused to fix her eyes on the couple, dancing again.

'Their name's *not* Rodgers by the way. Let me see, what is it – Harper? No – Hopkins? No – ah, yes, Hooper. Mr and Mrs Hooper.'

'*Very* interesting, my dear,' he drawled superiorly. 'I'm glad to find that your rather more laborious process has led you to discover exactly what I told you immediately on setting an eye on them. Hooper – Rodgers – of course, exactly the same name-pattern, don't you see? And – talking to them on the bus, you found them – how? Shall I tell you? Pleasant. Polite. Unworrying. Some remarks about the weather. What a nice hotel it is. Have you been here before – No, not here, but last year we went to Torquay – no, perhaps Weston-super-Mare. With the woman you exchanged some remarks about womanly things of even more doubtful importance. The man, slightly bored, sat silent most of the time, but occasionally, and with heavy politeness, he contributed a sentence or two. He probably said he liked a change. Yes, very probably ...'

As he spoke, he occasionally extracted a phrase or a sentence and docketed it away in a corner of his mind, for future usage.

'Come now, isn't that what happened?' he inquired coaxingly, bullying, of his wife, fastening his clear, rather cruel eyes upon her and causing her to blush and fluster.

'Oh, well really. I – it wasn't at all like that –'

She was confused because while he was talking her mind had flashed away to the couple; not as they were on the bus, but as she had observed them walking about the hotel – little things she had noted, though not formulated very clearly.

'They seem a nice young couple, Carlton,' she said, rather lamely. 'I will have to introduce you. They are here for a week.'

She paused. 'They come from London.'

He held up a hand, commandingly.

'Enough! There will be no need, I am glad to say, for you to bother with introductions. The mere fact that I am making a special study of the couple in question is quite enough to give me all the questions I am sure I would ever wish to have ...

'And London – of course, exactly as I forecast,' he went on, pleased. He began shaking his head as though in mild and sardonic pity.

'Human nature!' he exclaimed. 'Such a frightening jig-saw at first – such an easy jig-saw, later on! The prison of suburban life. The weak fluttering desire of the inmates to escape into something a little more bright and gay. Ah, how they struggle, how they flutter, weaker and weaker. But, of course, they make their small temporary escape. They taste the thrill – just a taste, mind you (how frightened they would be to really escape!) Oh, you may be sure, they keep their feet firmly on the ground ... The return ticket is in their pocket, the milkman has been told to resume deliveries in seven days' time – the escape is fitted so neatly into the routine.'

As he spoke she felt uneasy, knowing that when he spoke like this, his voice deepening in tone and rising in harshness, his face changed, began to take on the character you would expect from listening to the tone, brittle in its venom. The face tautened, became shaded with thick patches of dark brooding; the long veins in the neck coloured darker and throbbed, as if the savagery was being pumped up from mysterious depths through the neck and into the great, cavernous interior of the head. The eyes narrowed as if to focus their bright venom upon the particular object, and they seemed to see nothing else even if you could bear to meet them ... Knowing all this she looked away and watched the dancing, until he had finished and fallen into a morose silence.

'Are you writing, then – about them – this couple?' she asked timidly, at last.

He laughed, a hollow, affected sound.

'I suppose you might say so – possibly, I am wasting valuable time and talents on this dull and insipid couple. Yet perhaps it will be time and talents not entirely wasted. They make as good a prop as any, and certainly a good coconut shy.'

'Oh!' she said. She made a mute, fluttery protest with her hands; no more.

'How dull and stupid people seem to be,' he said mechanically, and he threw away the rolled-up piece of bread, watching it roll across the middle of the floor and being trampled into crumbs by the dancers.

With sudden relief she saw Mr Brailsford coming towards the table, eyebrows raised with their polite invitation to dance.

The next few days he spent most of his time at his writing desk, working on his story. His wife, never too sure of her health, rested on the settee, or slept a good deal. She wanted to be in good form for her first afternoon's help to Mrs Hemmings on the Friday. She was glad that Carlton was working and would probably be occupied during the time she would be absent.

116

In the afternoons, while Carlton steadily tapped away on his neat portable typewriter, she took gentle strolls in the rambling grounds of the hotel. Once, down by the boating-lake, she came upon the Hoopers. They had been for a walk across the pine-wood hills adjoining the grounds and their faces were flushed from the exercise. They smiled a greeting at her and she stood talking to them for a few moments, a rambling, inconsequential, rather pleasant conversation. Then they went down to the lake and took out one of the rowing boats. It rocked violently as they attempted to get in and she heard them laughing at each other's clumsiness. At last they pushed off, the man rowing with steady strokes, the woman leaning her head back and trailing her fingers in the water. She waved them good-bye and went back, smiling.

On the Friday there was a letter from Carlton Smithers' agent informing him that the film rights of his last novel had been sold for fifty thousand dollars. After a momentary pang of resentment at the thought of the liberal portion of that sum which would go into the totally unworthy pockets of the agent, he permitted himself a broad smile of satisfaction at this latest testimony to his success. Hollywood would make a catastrophic mess of the story, of course. Still, it would mean, in addition to the money, a whole horde of new cuttings and write-ups: 'I hear that the latest best-selling novel by Mr Carlton Smithers, the famous British novelist, is to be made into a film. I have it on good authority that the purchase price is one of Hollywood's highest ever.' Also, it would make a new feature in his conversation, solidifying his position as the star of the hotel's social life.

Feeling more alive than he had done for a long time he ate a large and satisfying breakfast and fixed a round of golf with Liefberg, a medium player whom he could usually be certain of beating. Besides, Liefberg was a man who appreciated the value of money. It was pleasing to hear his whistle of approbation upon the casual mention of the fifty thousand dollars' deal.

'We'll have to celebrate,' he told his wife jovially when he

117

got back to the hotel.

'Oh – well – ' She began to stutter, her hands fluttering nervously. Always fussing, he thought, with annoyance.

'Come, come, no arguing!' he directed, patting her reprovingly on the shoulder. 'It isn't every day that even Carlton Smithers sells a book for fifty thousand dollars. That's about twenty-nine thousand pounds, you know.'

'But –' She wanted to say something about Mrs Hemmings and the afternoon appointment. But in her nervousness she could not begin.

'That settles it, then,' he flashed, peremptorily. 'A nice lunch at the Bull, then a picture show. Back here for dinner, with an extra bottle of champagne – and I've fixed a nice bridge four with the Liefbergs, afterwards.'

'Not so bad, eh?' he said, pleased at his efficient planning. He began taking off his golfing clothes.

'How about putting on some glad rags, too?' he went on, eyeing his wife's familiar dress with distaste.

'Very well, dear.'

She sighed, and began to change, wondering worriedly how she would be able to let Mrs Hemmings know. There was, she discovered – as the day was swallowed up rapidly by the taxi ride, the huge meal, the drowsy cinema – no opportunity.

On the way back they both felt a little tired. He thought, rather irritably, what dull company she had been.

'By the way,' he said suddenly. 'Did you see the exciting and glamorous Rodgers – I mean, Hoopers?'

'No – ' she said, interested. 'What a pity we didn't speak to them ...

'Oh, dear,' she exclaimed suddenly, remembering something. 'And to-morrow's – ' She stopped, not wishing to kindle his resentment at them.

What she had been going to say was that tomorrow was the last day of their holiday.

'They really are pathetic,' he went on, staring haughtily out of the car window. 'They were walking down the hill and holding hands like a couple of juveniles. Sentimental tosh!'

As the result of the outing, the liberal meals, the cinema show, the champagne and an argumentative bridge party, he lay in bed the next morning, twisting and turning unhappily at the impact of sharp pains shooting about his nether regions. At each pain he gave a deep groan and an extravagant expression of his torture. He decided to stay in bed awhile and be looked after as befitted a bilious invalid.

His wife did not feel too well, either, but she dutifully got up and saw to it that his sheets were re-arranged, special glasses of warm milk fetched, the necessary pills and lotions put to hand. After slipping down for a cup of tea she came and sat down beside him all morning, attending to his wants, reading to him from the newspapers – twice refilling the two hot-water bottles that were soothing the disturbed stomach. Now and then she fidgeted and glanced at him, wondering if he were likely to drop asleep. Half-conscious of her impatience he seemed to force himself to keep awake, but just before lunch-time the bald head sank into the pillow and he dropped off.

On an impulse she decided to have her lunch downstairs: it always meant such a lot of fuss having lunch in the bedroom. After carefully instructing the housemaid to take up a light bread and milk lunch to Carlton, she went into the dining-room.

At the table she felt strange in her solitude, and noticed several curious eyes upon her. Unused to being the centre of attraction she blushed, wishing the table were in a less prominent position. Suddenly, seeing the Hoopers coming in at the doorway – and again on an impulse – she beckoned them over and inquired if they would care to join her. To her surprise, and pleasure, they did.

At first she wondered if there would be a shadow over this, their last day. But it was not at all like that. The conversation came smoothly and pleasantly, and as the lunch went on she felt they had known each other a long time, and were friends. She was genuinely sorry when the meal was over and it was time for them to get ready to depart. 'Good luck. Very good luck,' she said as they left her, feeling that it must sound empty and foolish; but meaning it.

He was standing at the window when she went back, later in the afternoon.

'Are you feeling better, dear,' she said, feeling rather guilty at her lengthy absence. He certainly looked better, and his eyes were brighter.

'So-so,' he said disdainfully. He inclined his head out of the window.

'I couldn't resist taking a farewell peep at our fascinating visitors. Here yesterday, gone to-day, thank goodness. I was getting bored in bed, anyway,' he said savagely. 'I decided to finish my story. Seeing the departure of the Hoopers stimulated my creative faculty, you might say.'

Still in his dressing-gown – a beautiful silk gown embroidered in gold and silver with a Chinese dragon – he went through and sat at his desk. A moment later she heard the typewriter. She lay down wearily on the bed and closed her eyes, listening to the words tapping out smoothly and resolutely, without any hesitation or doubt. Gradually the clatter sent her to sleep.

He awoke her, roughly, an hour later. He carried a sheaf of papers in his hand.

'Here,' he said, thrusting them before her still sleepy eyes. 'I've finished at last ... I thought it might amuse you to read the story.'

'Why, yes, of course, dear,' she said, automatically – as she had said it automatically at the invitation to read all the other stories. Only this time the words came back as echoes. Why – yes – of – course – dear – They rang hollow and unreal, and suddenly she knew that she did not want to read this particular story. Uneasily, she began to read.

He went back to the writing-desk, began clearing up the dishevelled papers. It had not been such a great effort as he would like to make out. There was a certain knack, a particular technique – an apt phrase here, a swift rapier thrust there. Long ago he had become master of them, they came to him almost as instincts, he supposed. He sorted the odd sheets of paper on which he had begun scribbling, then left off – sometimes a sentence, sometimes a paragraph. The notes he scribbled, but the stories he wrote straight on to the typewriter. Once he had decided on the basic element he found it simple to write the story. He seldom had need to correct. This was one of the rewards of patient diligent study of human nature, as he had no doubt pointed out in one of his books.

He was surprised to hear heavy breathing at the doorway. He looked round, startled. His wife was standing there, leaning to one side, her face white, but with two pinpoints of red burning in each cheek. She held the manuscript tightly, crumpled in one hand.

'Why – what on earth?' Suddenly he felt incapable of getting out of his seat.

'The story – ' he began, protestingly.

'Take your story!' She threw it forward, on to the floor. 'I've read it. From beginning to end. Oh, I've read it! So accomplished. So shrewd. So clever. So pointedly drawn from life. Oh, yes – ' She gave a strange laugh. 'I've read your little satire on the Hoopers. Oh, Carlton!' Her harsh voice broke into something softer, pleading; a voice heavy with ancient sorrow. 'You fool! Oh, you fool!' she sobbed, rather to his surprise.

'Fool?'

She took a step forward, staring at him anguishedly, then shaking her head.

'Does it never occur to you, Carlton, that the world is sometimes a little bigger, a little different, to the neat precise picture you frame on your neat white sheet of paper? Do you never consider the possibility that the suits you so cleverly and assuredly place upon so many different shoulders may not always fit?'

She took a deep breath.

'In case it interests you,' she went on, her voice rising to an unexpected fury of sound, 'Mr and Mrs Hooper are a man

121

and a woman. A decent good man and a decent good woman. And they're in love, and extremely happy. It doesn't matter at all where they come from or where they may be going to. It doesn't matter at all whether he jingles pounds or pennies in his pockets, neither does it matter whether she does the washing on Monday or Tuesday or any other day. None of these things matter, because when a man and woman are in love and happy, they carry their life with them and they are whole and complete.

'Can't you see?' she cried. 'They are not to be pitied or despised, far less made fun of – why, they are to be *envied* from the bottom of our hearts!'

She paused, exhausted, conscious of his hypnotised stare. She suddenly saw, silhouetted, his long wrinkled face, creased by his life and behaviour – his malevolence and his cruelty – into a permanent, irremovable mask. Through the slits she met the eyes; they were extraordinarily blank, and quite dry.

'Oh, but – ' she said despairingly. 'You would never understand. I see now – forty years – You never did – You never will ...

'Never!' she cried, throwing her hands into the air in a hopeless gesture. And she turned and ran out of the room as if it was the end of her life; which it was.

'Well! Well, indeed!' he exclaimed, while he struggled to maintain his composure. Then:

'Why,' he said. 'Why, what a wonderful story this would make!' – and he began running his long curved finger down the side of his protruding nose, looking down thoughtfully at the waiting heap of neat white paper.

VI

This Year, Next Year

Ironically, it was her husband who made the suggestion in the first place.

'Look, it's going to be pretty boring for you during the next few months with me working late every night on the scheme ... you've always wanted to follow up your interest in pottery. Why don't you start going to evening classes? It'll help to pass the time.'

It was true about 'the scheme' – sometimes Nell hated the sound of the word, for somehow already the venture seemed to have come between her and Peter. Of course, she quite understood the importance to a young architect of a chance to draw up complete plans for this vast new modern hotel. If it was a success then undoubtedly there would be further commissions and Peter would be able to set up on his own account. No, she could not honestly begrudge him the fulfilment of such a dream, and yet ... She was beginning to hate those long evenings when Peter gave an apologetic smile and went off to shut himself up in his workroom for several hours. It wasn't much fun watching television on her own night after night, or trying to concentrate on a book. And really, if she went on like this she knew she would end up taking it out on Peter.

'All right,' she found herself agreeing. 'You're probably right. I'll go along to the local tech and see what's doing.'

She found there was quite a lot doing at the local tech,

almost a bewilderment of classes, with pottery high on the popularity list. Indeed it was only because she had studied pottery before and could reasonably join a class half way through a session that she was accepted for enrolment, and told to come along the following Wednesday.

When she arrived on the appointed evening she was rather amused to see so many married women of about her own age eagerly attending, and had a comic vision of dozens of dutiful husbands sitting at home minding things. But of course, though she smiled she was soon impressed by the industrious way everyone set to – and inevitably, after a while, imbued with the same sort of enthusiasm. She had forgotten how satisfying it was to handle the soft pliable red clay, to pick up the lumps of apparently inanimate material and slowly fashion them into something living.

It was a long time since she had actually handled clay and she was only modelling it, as a child might do, but there was something about the way she tackled the job that must have caught the instructor's eye, for he came and stood beside her, nodding approvingly.

'I can see you've worked with clay before.'

'Yes, some years ago I used to go to classes. I only got so far, and then – well, I got married, and somehow dropped it.'

'And what's made you take it up again?'

She hadn't meant to go into personal details, but somehow before the evening was out she found herself explaining the whole story of Peter's scheme, and her own growing sense of frustration. It wasn't so much that she was a garrulous gossip, but rather something to do with the quiet, almost reserved personality of the instructor. His name was Mike Robson, and he was a tall, rather aesthetic-looking man with a dark, almost saturnic face which seemed to exude a quality of brooding watchfulness. He seemed very much a lonely figure, not the sort of man, she would have thought, to find communication easy. But somehow she was not conscious of any barrier herself and in fact they talked so animatedly that most of the others had gone before she realised how late it was.

124

'You've been very kind,' she said, getting ready to go. 'I mean, sparing so much time to attend to my problems.'

When he smiled, then, she was surprised how much younger he looked, and indeed, drawn by the strange brightness of his eyes.

'That's what I'm here for.'

'Yes, but … ' She hesitated, and then found herself smiling back. 'Well, anyway, I'm grateful.'

He nodded as she turned: and all the way down the long classroom towards the exit she had a persistent impression that he might be watching her. So strong was the feeling that just at the doorway she could not resist turning to look. He was, indeed, standing by his desk, looking in her direction … On seeing her turn, he raised a hand in a curious, rueful gesture of farewell.

She went away thinking, not as she might have imagined, about her lessons; but, more precisely, about her teacher. She could not forget the way in which he had watched her, as if in some way by her departure he was left very much alone. She remembered from what he had told her that he did apparently live alone, and wondered if he was really a lonely man.

When she got home Peter was sitting by the fire, dozily.

'Hullo, how did it go?'

'All right.'

'Good.'

He said no more, and she thought, with growing anger, he really isn't interested. A strange, subterranean kind of antagonism was born … and to alleviate it she began looking forward to her next class.

The next week when she came she asked if she could have a turn on the potter's wheel.

'Yes, of course. Have you thrown before?'

'We-ell, just a little.'

'In that case perhaps I'd better demonstrate first.'

He sat himself at the wheel, picked up a large ball of prepared clay, centred it, and switched the electric wheel into

125

action. As soon as the blob was spinning round at a fair pace he lifted up his hands and plunged them expertly into the heart of the whirling clay. For a while it seemed as if nothing was happening, and then gradually he seemed to smooth the clay down and then, inexorably, to pull it outwards ... then, with another swift gesture he cupped the clay between his palms and began lifting up the walls, forming the cylindrical outside shape of a pot.

She watched in fascination, as much intrigued by the performance as by the result. In particular she kept watching Mike Robson's hands – they seemed to become living things, as they sank deep into the red clay. They were long, slender yet immensely strong hands; in their way, rather beautiful. It seemed to her they must reflect something of the man himself.

'Oh, dear,' she said, when the demonstration was over. 'I'll never be able to do anything like that.'

'Of course you will. Here, have a try.'

She climbed on to the wheel, drew up the sleeves of her dress, and picked up a ball of clay. Meantime Mike Robson stood close beside her, showing her how to position herself.

'Don't go stiff and rigid like so many students do. Just hold yourself relaxed ... that's right. Now then, start the wheel and practise first of all centring the clay.'

It seemed to her that she spent most of the evening at the wheel, and this must be unfair to the other students, but at the same time Mike Robson appeared so engrossed in imparting to her some of his technique that she did not dare to interrupt him. She found herself, anyway, intrigued by the capacity he obviously had for completely immersing himself in whatever task engaged his interest. He was, there was no doubt about it, a very interesting man. And, she thought, not altogether casually, a very attractive one.

After the class had finished and she was collecting her things he came over for a moment.

'Well now, it wasn't so very difficult, was it?'

'No, thanks to you. You're very kind.'

He shrugged. 'It's my job.'

126

She looked at him curiously.

'Have you always been a teacher?'

He smiled, and once again she was startled by the transformation from an almost sullen look to an appearance of brightness and youth. It seemed to her that such a radical transformation must run through his whole personality.

'I only teach part-time here, you know. I have my own pottery at home.' He paused and looked at her gravely, in a silence which lasted so long that she became almost self-conscious of the moments passing, as if they were very significant ones.

'You must come out and see it some time,' he said quietly.

At first she did not pay much attention to the remark. But then as the weeks slowly went by and her regular visits to the pottery classes began to assume a disturbing significance, so she found herself remembering the moment, the words – the curious gesture, almost of resignation, as if somehow he had been trapped into saying something he had never meant to say.

Sometimes, during the interval between one class and another, she tried to analyse the subtle relationship that was inexorably being created. Mike Robson never outwardly revealed any more personal interest in her than any of his other students. Towards them all he had a gentle, understanding sort of approach which she could see was widely appreciated. And yet, somehow she could not rid herself of a secret knowledge that, despite all this, there was some strange link between the two of them.

It was a problem that confused her quite a little: if it had been any other kind of problem she would have liked to talk it over with Peter. But then Peter, anyway, was increasingly immersed in his beloved scheme. Night after night he remained locked in his workroom not merely for an hour or two, but often until after midnight. Sometimes when he emerged, blinking, looking strained and tired, she felt a terrible urge to comfort him, to take him in her arms ... the

127

sad thing was that the continual separation was taking its toll, sometimes they seemed almost like strangers, and so she found it impossible to make even a simple gesture.

Instead, she went along to the next class possessed by a kind of recklessness. It was not her custom to bother unduly about her appearance for an evening's pottery class, but on this occasion she made herself up carefully, as if going out for an evening. It was, she supposed, as much to give herself confidence as anything else; but the fact was she looked very smart and attractive, she knew, and the effect was not lost on Mike Robson.

By now she had become quite an accomplished thrower and she was left to work largely on her own. But this evening, as if drawn despite himself, Mike came and stood watching her.

'You're getting along famously ... A credit to your instructor, eh?'

She turned and looked at him searchingly, a bold look which she might not have dared under other circumstances.

'In that case,' she said firmly, 'perhaps I could take you up on that invitation to visit your pottery?'

She travelled over one spring afternoon early the next week. The small cottage where he lived was on the other side of the town, beyond even the suburban environs. She got off the bus at the corner and followed his instructions to aim for the last building at the end of a winding country lane. All the way out, on the bus, even starting down the lane, she had been caught up as if by a sense of adventure ... Now, as she stepped over the threshold of the garden gate and so entered his unknown world, too late she knew this to be alarmingly more than an ordinary adventure.

'Hullo.' He had seen her coming, appeared now at the door of a small workshop adjoining the cottage. Already, in this private setting, he seemed different from the college. For one thing he did not wear the usual standard overalls, but just jeans and an open-necked red shirt, the casual attire lending him a youthful zest.

For a moment he stood smiling warmly at her, as if in some way he could not quite believe she had come: then he beckoned her in and for the next half hour showed her round the orderly routine of his pottery studio. When he came to the massive old-fashioned kick-wheel she asked shyly if he would throw a pot, and without a word he picked up some clay and began to throw. Deep down inside of her she knew that part of her reason for asking was the rather sensual one of repeating the pleasure she always felt at the sight of those delicate hands, moulding and shaping the clay into life. Somehow, in this unfamiliar setting, the sensation was more vivid than ever, and she could not stop staring at the hands ... perhaps this upset his concentration, for half way through he spoiled the pot and it collapsed.

'Oh, dear,' she began apologetically. 'I'm sorry ...'

Without a word he picked up another ball and started throwing again. This time she held her breath and hardly looked and he completed the pot successfully. Then, as he lifted it gingerly and put it on a board to dry off, he said:

'There, that shall be a present for you. I'll glaze and fire it and bring it along to the next class.'

Touched, she bent down and looked at the pot, still wet with the spiral thread of his finger pressure – suddenly it seemed to mark, as some kind of solid and irrevocable thing, a bond between them.

'Well,' he said, swinging his tall frame off the wheel. 'What do you think of my little workshop?'

'I envy you ... it's so well organised.' She hesitated, and then looked beyond to the cottage. 'And you live here all alone?'

'Yes. Come along, I'll make you a cup of tea.'

She followed him into the snug lounge, and they settled there while they waited for the kettle to boil. At first their talking together seemed amusing and even strangely intimate: but then gradually she became aware of some constraint in the air. Once or twice, turning, she was disturbed to find his eyes resting upon her quite fiercely.

'Why do you look like that?' she said at last.

'How do you mean?'

'As if – why, as if you've never seen me before.'

He laughed.

'Perhaps in a way I haven't. After all, you must admit that usually you're safely hidden behind an old overall. And now!'

'Yes,?' she said, savouring the strange pleasure. 'And now?''

'Now,' he said with a quiet intensity, 'you seem to light up the cottage.' He gave a curious laugh. 'I suppose it's been dark too long.'

They went through the motions of having their cups of tea and continuing to exchange comparatively small talk. But all the time the real issues simmered below. At last, agitated, perhaps afraid, she blurted out almost defiantly:

'It's late – I'll have to be going.'

She turned to get her things, but not before she had seen the hurt look in his eyes.

'Must you go – so soon?'

'I'm afraid so. You see ... Well ... ' She spread her hands in a helpless gesture.

As she put on her coat and prepared to go she kept telling herself that these were decisive actions, the completion of a harmless excursion. And all the time he stood at the other side of the room by the front door, just watching.

'Well,' she said awkwardly, moving towards the door. 'Thank you so much for showing me the pottery. I've enjoyed it very much.'

Somehow she managed to walk past him and out of the front door and down the narrow garden path ... she remembered afterwards, oddly, smelling the hyacinths lining the hedges and the distant honeysuckle. But then a strange thing happened, as she went to open the gate ... her footsteps seemed to falter, of their own volition. Try as she would she found she could not walk any further.

For a moment, confused, she stood where she was. Then, turning, she saw him still standing at the doorway, as if he, too, had not moved – could not have moved.

130

She looked back, tears in her eyes.

'Mike ...'

And then she found herself running, as if it was the most urgent of all journeys possible – back along the garden path and into his waiting embrace.

It was an hour at least before finally she left. During that time they had moved into the sitting room and sat side by side on the velvet-lined couch, looking at one another wonderingly. Now and then he would put out a hand and touch her hair, and sometimes she rubbed his cheek. But otherwise they hardly spoke: there was really no need for words. There was just something existing between them, which had secretly existed for some time ... and now, irrevocably, was publicly proclaimed.

'I'm sorry,' he began once, troubled.

She put a finger to his lips.

'It's nobody's fault.'

She paused, trying to think back clearly. 'It's a funny thing but –'

She had been going to comment on the fact it had been her husband who had persuaded her to attend the classes, but thought better of it.

'I suppose – ' She shrugged. 'I suppose it was meant.'

Meant or not, the reality and strength of their unexpected love affair was disturbing. At first she convinced herself that her feeling for Mike Robson was mainly a protective one: after all, his life was a solitary one. It was almost as if perversely he had shut himself off into a world of his own. She guessed, but did not press the subject, that at some time he had been hurt in some way by a woman – and perhaps this awareness, too, helped her to bridge the gap in communication.

But somehow, once she had done that, she could almost have wished to step back, a little afraid at the flood-tide let loose. It was as if everything inside him that had been pent-up poured out unchecked.

'You know, I think I fell in love with you that very first

evening,' he said, lying beside her, propped up on one elbow, staring down at her with his deep brown eyes.

'Why?'

He stared at her, baffled.

'I don't know ...'

And then, reminding her of some youthful knight errant of other days, he bent forward and encompassed her, his lips meeting hers hungrily. At such moments all her instinctive feelings of panic seemed to vanish, overwhelmed by her body's instinctive response.

She knew in her heart that they could not help themselves. Otherwise she, for one, would have tried to avert what was happening. As it was they settled into a strange half unreal existence, living on borrowed time. As long as her husband was so engrossed in his beloved scheme it was possible to equate the deception with a kind of normality. She had let it be known she was attending two evening classes a week, and this gave them a precious evening to themselves. Usually she caught the bus over to Mike's cottage and they spent a quiet domestic evening together, at one with each other, content. Once or twice they risked meeting in the daytime, but such meetings were always conditioned by secret fears of discovery.

There was one exception, though, when they caught a train out to a small market town and then walked up on to the wind-blown downs. There, walking hand in hand, the sun beating down upon them and the world around like a heavenly fairyland, they felt very close.

'Nell,' he said in a strange voice. 'Supposing things had been different, supposing we had met a long time ago ... would you have married me?'

She pressed his hand. There was no difficulty in replying.

'Yes ... yes, I would.'

And somehow, she felt, no disloyalty, either. It was Peter she was married to, but there was only one life, who could say how many loves hovered on the horizon? How could one possibly ever know? If she had never gone to the pottery classes, never met Mike, she would never have known about

132

him. And yet now here he was beside her, real, alive, beloved. In some way, deep down, she found it hard to feel it very wrong to love someone.

They went on climbing, right up to the top of the wide sweeping downs ... and there on the top they lay on the soft turf, staring up at the sun, holding hands, unable to speak, clasped together by a tremulous emotion of lovingness.

After a while they drew closer. She felt, burningly, the sudden touch of his hands – remembered them in their delicate beauty and pressed them hard against her soft flesh, aware of a moment of indescribable ecstasy in their strange communion.

'My darling,' she whispered to the wind.

And there somehow, in the carefree sunshine, on that magical day, it seemed to her that they entered into a realm beyond ordinary criticism; a secret place of their own, which would always belong to just the two of them. And which she could never, never regret.

Curiously – perhaps typically – the moment of perfection also marked a point of separation. It was nothing either of them could put a finger upon, but the awareness was there.

About this time Nell noticed that Peter seemed to have come to the end of his task. Or at least, he seemed suddenly to be restless and more visible. One evening he surprised her by not retiring to his workroom, but coming to sit by the fire.

'Have you a class tonight?'

She flushed.

'Why, yes, I'm afraid so.'

'Oh, never mind.' He looked somewhat crestfallen. 'I just thought ...'

'Oh, well,' she began, but he made a gesture of dismissal.

'No, no – you go along.' He paused. 'How's it going, by the way?'

She looked up, perturbed, but saw nothing untoward in his expression.

'Oh, quite well, really.'

133

'Why don't you bring home some pots?'

She nodded, dumbly.

"All right, I will.'

When she returned, she did bring one or two of her pots. Peter picked them up and stood them under the light, studying them with great concentration. All at once she began to feel uneasy. Was it possible – could he possibly suspect something? But no, it was impossible.

'These are good,' he said, seemingly in surprise. 'Really good.'

He smiled at her approvingly. 'You've done well.'

There was a faint pause, and then:

'You must have a good instructor.'

She tried not to hear the sudden pounding of her heart. It was horrible to feel like this, so guilty and ashamed; yet why should she be surprised?

Later that night, lying in bed unable to sleep, she went over and over the conversation, trying to read into it perhaps more than there was. After all, Peter couldn't possibly know ... and yet ... Supposing he had found out something, supposing suddenly he taxed her with it ... What would she feel? How would she explain?

She knew, somehow, it would be impossible. And better for all concerned if she never had to. Troubled, she turned over and tried to fall asleep; but sleep was a long time coming.

The next evening when she came home she was surprised to find Peter there waiting for her. He looked a little sheepish, and said:

'I finished early today. I thought maybe we'd eat out for a change. What do you say?'

She accepted quite gladly, aware guiltily of the lack of a problem because it was not one of her evenings at the college. She and Peter went into town and ate at a little Italian restaurant familiar from the old days of their first year together. It was an odd, relaxed evening, she felt pleased not to have to think about anything, just relax. Peter, too, seemed more at ease. On the way home she found herself linking arms with him, feeling a surge of affection that had been too long dimmed.

'That was nice,' she said, when they got home. 'Let's do it again.'

The next evening when she was at the pottery class and vividly aware of Mike Robson staring over at her from time to time, she wondered if she was being an outrageous hypocrite. What on earth was happening to her? One moment she had been a meek little suburban wife, watching the television every night – now she was a woman with two men in her life, strangely drawn to both of them.

At his request she lingered behind till the other students had gone. When she had washed and changed he came and looked at her anxiously.

'Don't you realise this is the last class of the term? If you hadn't stayed – how would I have got in touch with you?'

He smiled, and she had not the heart to tell him of the momentary feeling that had come over – a wish that indeed she had gone, and the problem could thus have been avoided.

'Well,' he went on, 'when shall we meet?'

Weakly, she agreed to meet on the forthcoming afternoon. Once again they went off to the country ... but this time things seemed different. Because, she supposed, she was different. It was nothing that anyone had said or done – certainly not Peter nor Mike – just something inside of her that had given way, so that she no longer felt able to cope.

All the way home she pondered upon what to do. Her problems were momentarily shelved by the shock of finding Peter already home. He looked tired and confessed that he had been sent home to have a rest.

'They seem to think I've been overworking.'

'And so you have.' Scoldingly, she took charge: packed him off to bed, brought him a hot drink, sat by his side talking quietly until he began to doze off. Just before this, he turned and said curiously:

'Where have you been, by the way?'

'Oh,' she said vaguely. 'Just out for a walk ...'

He fell asleep then, and for some time she stayed there, studying the familiar face. It was a handsome face, but also – she realised perhaps for the first time – a rather weak face: the face of a man who *needed* a partner. Vaguely, half dozing herself, she super-imposed another face upon that – a lean, angular, less familiar face of someone who seemed by comparison much stronger, much less in need.

But was that really so? How could she know? All that week she tried to focus her mind upon the problem, and all the time it seemed to slide away.

During the holidays she saw Mike twice more. The first time it rained heavily and they spent most of the time enclosed in a tiny steaming teashop, arguing unfamiliarly, almost bickering, like an old married couple. As they came out she became overwhelmed by a feeling she was going to burst into tears, and only managed to hold them back with a tremendous effort. For suddenly she saw the future stretching ahead of her in a series of such encounters, continual surgings up and down of the human spirit. And knew it would be unendurable.

They met once again. This time the sun shone, and as if perhaps both aware of the importance of the occasion, they took a bus down to the seaside and strolled along wide stretches of white, bleached sands. They did not speak much but felt very close – it was almost, though not quite, like that marvellous day on the downs. In the gathering dusk of evening they walked back slowly towards the distant bus station, holding hands, enveloped, oh so briefly, by the immortal cloak of their strange companionship.

She did not see him again. When the time came for the start of the new term she did not re-apply. When her husband came home that evening, she tried to explain.

'But why stop now? You were doing so well.'

'Yes, I know. But ... well, I just don't want to carry on.'

Her husband did not say anything then. For a while he went into his workroom, and for one wild, disappointed moment she was afraid he was going back to 'the scheme'. But then he came out and shut the door behind him firmly. Then, smiling softly, he came and sat beside her in front of the fire they had lit – the first of an early winter.

'Well, I can't say I'm sorry, really.'

He looked at her shrewdly, and once again, fleetingly, she wondered if perhaps he knew more than she imagined. He put an arm round her shoulder.

'There's nothing like a cosy evening by the fire ... ' He paused and went on, a little huskily. ' ... with the woman you love.'

It sounded, in retrospect, almost banal. But somehow, not at the time. They sat there for quite a long time, while the fire burned up brighter and brighter ... and staring into the leaping flames she fancied she saw the consummation of something that might have been very precious, even if unattainable. But then, a little while later, as they both leaned forward and warmed themselves before the now well-established glow, she felt a strange sense of release. And almost of beginning again.

'Peter, dear,' she said softly, and began fondling his hair. 'My dearest Peter ...'

While he for his part, indeed much more aware than she could possibly have supposed, could only be thankful, deep in his heart, that it was all over at last: and that a second chance must gratefully be taken.

VII

The Wound

The woman was beautiful but pregnant – heavily pregnant. It was a pregnancy not so much physically as almost spiritually obtrusive: its existence pervaded everything about the woman, even her very beauty. It was not that the pregnancy marred her beauty – rather it enhanced it, but in an unbearably poignant way. See, the swollen body seemed to cry out, see how beautiful I am, and how trapped. Admire me, yes – but, oh, pity me, I cannot escape, I am so helpless, what can I do? And across the lovely calm face, sometimes, there would flit the mere ghost of a smile that might have been.

The man with her was neat, dapper, almost exquisitely fashioned, with the tapering body of an athlete and the romantic good looks of youth – yet quietly, confidently, the father of her child. It might have been read in the almost insolent ease of his bearing – or, more readily, in the woman's face every time she turned to look at him, eyes widening, lips parting, in her face the shadow of despair, the light of love. Indeed, the woman's face mirrored, hauntingly, all the man's elusive, maddening charms.

They made an attractive couple: were the envy, as the saying goes, of all eyes. They were staying by the sea at a quiet hotel, a brief holiday, apparently, before returning wherever their home might be for the long-awaited event. Every morning they set off with a picnic box, taking the path down to the rocks, where seagulls wheeled in continual chatter above the swirling Atlantic waves.

It was in this fashion we met, for it was my custom to walk along the same path. At first we exchanged polite greetings and no more, but then gradually, perhaps because we were almost the only visitors at that out-of-season time, there developed between us a curious sort of intimacy – or perhaps I should say they admitted me into their intimacy. At least, I supposed so, since their lives certainly seemed closely interwoven. Every gesture, every sentence, seemed supercharged with secret meaning, known only to them. If the woman glanced away the man would demand, almost sharply, at what she glanced: if on the other hand, as often happened, he appeared lost in mysterious thoughts, the woman's lovely face would be clouded until he had revealed his secret experience. Yes, a very close union.

It was only, as I say, as I became part of the circle that hints of their real relationship became apparent. Nothing startling, nothing melodramatic – only quite deadly.

'Joanna,' he said dreamily one day, as we stared over the water, 'what would you do if I was unfaithful to you?'

I glanced quickly at Joanna, realising from her protective expression that she had heard the question many times before.

'You know what I would do,' she said dully. 'I would leave you.'

But somehow there was no force in her tone, no meaning in her words: and the man knew it. Indeed he laughed, as if with sheer delight. When he laughed, his young face became younger, his romantic looks even more romantic. Joanna bit her lip tightly, and looked away, her cheeks flushed. I felt a little uncomfortable and wished the man would stop talking.

'Do you remember in London, Joanna?' he went on softly. 'Wasn't I unfaithful to you then? Why didn't you leave me then, eh?'

This time the woman shrugged, perhaps tossed her head, like a proud stallion, and met his eyes. I saw that hers were dark and full of strange beauty, like mysterious jewels – but alas, so were his.

'I don't care about the past,' she said; her whole being expressing, helplessly, that she did.

The young man, Tony was his name, lay back and stared up at the sky. His face in profile was almost unbearably beautiful: even as I watched the woman bent forward and lightly touched his cheek with her fingers.

'Don't let's quarrel ...'

Suddenly Tony turned over on his stomach, quickly, venomously, like a snake.

'Ah, but you *always* say that, don't you? Don't let's quarrel, don't let's argue, don't let's do or be ... you just want us to live in a vacuum, but life isn't like that. Is it?' he added, appealing for a moment to me.

I shook my head, refusing to be drawn. But I did remark, after a while, that Joanna's baby must soon be due.

'Ah,' said Tony scornfully. 'The great defence mechanism ... pregnancy protection, inc ... And so do you think – ' He stared pointedly, almost accusingly at his wife. '– Do you think for one moment that it is good that I should feel tied to you, like a dog, just by a physical weakness?'

Joanna looked curiously tired, her face seeming to sag.

'I don't think that.'

'Ah, but really you do. Deep down you want to own me, to hold me forever in those possessive hands of yours ...'

His voice went on, but I only half listened, as the rest of me watched Joanna. Her face was like a mask, and yet the sort of mask through which one could see everything. At each word which Tony uttered it was as if some invisible dagger sank in, deep down, to the very heart. After a while, perhaps the blood congealed, the sores merged into one larger, more diffused ache – that, at least, I hoped.

It was the first of many such experiences. After a while, I think, they came to accept my presence as even a contribution to their endless, underground warfare. I was, at the last, an audience. Sometimes, indeed, Tony would appeal to me, unnecessary as that might seem. It was part of his volatility that he should suddenly turn and demand some comment from me: he was all movement and energy and life, a secretive and rather magic sort of life. It was impossible not to respond to his charm, his attraction. He was, perhaps, like the sun which draws, even though it burns.

Sometimes it would appear that he was teasing:

'Did you notice that I was a long time getting the papers this morning, Joanna? Ah now, I wonder what I was up to, eh? Perhaps I was flirting with the girl in the shop, you know the one with the slanting eyes and the way of walking.'

But, subtly, one became aware it was more than teasing. He *had* been a long time, he *did* flirt with the girl, and she *had* got slanting eyes and a way of walking ... All these things were known only too well to Joanna: how could she be sure, then?

'Ah, but how can you be sure?' Tony's voice echoed, sometimes indeed seeming to re-echo among the lonely rocks.

Once, only once, I ventured a comment to Joanna. Tony had gone for a swim among the rocks that jutted out here and there for some way into the ocean. As he slid into the water, his dark hair suddenly floating out like a weed, he seemed almost to become some creature of the sea: perhaps a man mermaid, I thought, half amused. Yes, I thought, continuing the idea, in many ways Tony did seem out of the human world, somehow elemental, so that perhaps he did not have human reactions so obviously. Perhaps he did not mean, or at least even know that he was so cruel, so malicious to his wife? All the same ...

'I don't think,' I began, watching the ephemeral form vanishing and re-appearing in the green waters, 'Tony means half the things he says. I mean, I'm sure he's really devoted –'

I stopped, aware of Joanna all tensed up beside me. Suddenly she grasped my arm and dug her fingers in, and then I felt the pressure relax.

142

'Oh, God ... I thought he'd never come up. Didn't you see? He nearly drowned ... Oh, thank God!'

I turned and stared after the elusive form, weaving in and out among the rocks, completely sure, cold-blooded efficient: then I looked, a little amazed, at Joanna's face, still half-afraid, the eyes still bright with unquenched fear. I shrugged.

'I expect he'll be all right.'

I began to wonder if I should give up my walks, so as to avoid these meetings: yet I could not quite bring myself to do so. Perhaps it was curiosity, perhaps a quixotic feeling of protection towards Joanna, perhaps – who knows? It might even have been a kind of morbidity on my own part, a desire to follow crime through to its inevitable end, as it seemed to me. The crime of killing the spirit of another human being.

As Joanna grew nearer to her time, so that her movements became heavier, her bearing more ponderous, Tony seemed to delight, with deceptive casualness, in commenting on the pleasing and by comparison effortless physical movements of other women.

'Do you remember, Joanna, when you were like that? When we were young and gay, tra-la-la ... Yes, my sweet, you, too, could have a figure like that ... and will again one day I suppose. Yes ... I wonder where we'll be, eh, Joanna? Do you think we'll still be together? Do you think you'll still have me prisoner in your arms? I wonder, eh?'

And as he lay, propped up on one elbow, eyebrows raised in the endless question, one could momentarily surmise that this was the whole of life to Tony; and endless question, a perpetual relentless wondering – a progress towards what?

I shall never know, I suppose. A day or so before my own departure we decided for a change to take a walk along the cliff paths which meandered high above the Atlantic waves, so that we seemed curiously remote and cut off. It was a beautiful day, the sky was one vast blue dome, and the sun shone clear and pure, and one would have imagined everything would be at peace.

But, somehow, these very conditions always seemed to provoke Tony into fresh and more extravagant outbursts of malice. Or at least ... I suppose it was malice. Or could it – I wonder, could it have been a sort of love?

After walking some while we went and sat on a grassy mound, on the edge of a steep grassy slope. The air was scented with the smell of sea pinks and heather; a haze hung over the sea. We sat and dreamed our dreams.

'You know,' said Tony, turning to me for a moment with a deceiving smile, 'I almost wish you weren't going. We shall miss our audience, won't we, Joanna?'

It was then, just as I was about to try and match this typically sardonic remark, that it happened. For some reason, perhaps because she suddenly felt too hot or uncomfortable, Joanna decided to move. She half rose, turned on the steep path, and began to topple sideways. At the last moment, in desperation, she flung out one hand to catch the sharp edge of a granite stone – an effort that saved her from falling, at the cost of a jagged cut in her hand.

For a moment I remember witnessing the scene like some cameo that was suspended in mid-air, as if forever: Joanna half leaning over, and her long white arm suddenly spurting with red blood – and Tony, head half-turned in startled amazement, and those brown eyes opening more wide than ever I had seen them ...

And then, in a mysterious moment, the static scene was ended: with a leap Tony was at Joanna's side, a handkerchief out, binding the wound, murmuring to her, suddenly enveloping her in his arms, gently stemming the blood, a look of anguish and utter pity on his face.

'My baby,' he was saying, 'my poor darling baby, don't worry – there now, see, I've stopped the bleeding – oh, my poor little girl, don't worry – it'll be all right, just you see. There now, rest your head and I'll hold you tight. My poor little baby ...'

It was almost unnecessary for me to glance, as I did, at Joanna. Upon that lovely face was a look that I can only

144

describe as one of complete and utter happiness. It was the look of a woman contented and fulfilled to a point beyond which there is no return. There was really nothing I could do but quietly steal away.

VIII

The Haunting of Angela Prendergast

Angela Prendergast, although blessed with a certain dark, rather meek attractiveness, was a shy and somewhat introverted young woman. Brought up as an only child in a lonely and remote country vicarage she had, over the years, acquired just the sort of characteristics to be expected: she was fussy, inclined to be nervous, something of a hypochondriac, and in general the slave of a vivid and fanciful imagination.

It was this imagination, she kept telling herself firmly, that was responsible for the state of apprehension in which she now found herself, living all on her own in the large rambling house which had been left to her after the unfortunate demise of her parents. There was, no doubt about it – there was something faintly yet unmistakably wrong.

The trouble had begun – well, she could remember exactly, really. It had been one of those cold crisp February mornings, when despite a preliminary flickering of sunshine the temperature remained low enough to discourage leaving the cosy warmth of bed. In any case Angela had long ago evolved a spinsterish solution to the problem by leaning out and pressing the switch of the electric fire – then remaining snugly under the bedclothes until the room was decently warmed.

On this particular morning she recollected quite clearly how she had finally turned back the bedclothes and stepped out on to the softness of the sheepskin rug which had been a present to herself out of her inheritance. Standing up, she

147

yawned and stretched herself, then casually dropped off her nightdress and stood there, reflectively, eyeing her familiar image in the full length mirror on the wall opposite. Seen thus Angela Prendergast presented a rather charming picture of a still youthful woman, indeed physically in her prime, with the sort of willowy contours that would have done justice to an artist's model – though, of course, a girl as shy and reserved as Angela would have died rather than subjected herself to such a fate. However, here in the utter privacy of her own bedroom Angela often felt herself free of many inhibitions and took quite a pleasure in parading around in the state God originally made her ... examining herself with a sharp but not displeased eye.

It was whilst indulging in this harmless conceit, on that cool February morning, that Angela Prendergast had first experienced the strange qualm of apprehension, soon to become more familiar. For, just as she executed a charming pirouette in front of her mirror and then bowed down with exquisite grace, as any ballet dancer might have done – so, hauntingly, as if carried by a passing wind, she caught a tiny and undoubtedly alien sound. It was – well, it might have been – but then, how could it be? – all the same, there could be little doubt, for there was really no more exact description – yes, it was a sound very much like a sigh, a long drawn-out, rather sad sort of sigh.

Angela's immediate and very proper reaction was to utter a startled cry and, so to speak, hug herself to herself. Indeed, she remained frozen into this pose for quite some moments while, fearfully, she strained her ears to catch a repetition of the disturbing, intrusive sound. It was only as the usual silence persisted, markedly unbroken, that gradually she relaxed enough to be able to turn and grab some clothes and hastily cover her exposed condition.

Not that there was anyone to see such a private sight – of course not. Why, as soon as she was decent again Angela gathered her courage together and searched the room thoroughly from end to end. She opened the wardrobe, she

148

pulled out drawers, she drew back the curtains, she even peeped into the clothes basket. The only thing she did not do – but then what spinster could be expected to? – was to lie down and peep under the bed itself.

It took Angela quite a while to get over such a disturbing start to the day. After all, what could it have been? A puff of wind? Some falling plaster? Perhaps – horror of horrors! – a tiny mouse? Or ... what? Angela allowed herself to conjure up every possibility except the one outrageous one: that she saved for a more secret savouring. After all – well, who could begrudge a spinster her fantasies?

By nightfall Angela had recovered some of her composure and was back into her normal routine. She cooked a simple supper, ate it by the fire, and afterwards, reclining comfortably on the big leather couch, watched television. She liked television because it offered a romantic escape from the harsh, dull realities of everyday life: as a solitary escapist she had little difficulty in plunging into the celluloid dramas.

It was in the middle of one of these episodes that, for the second time that day, Angela scented something amiss. Or rather this time almost *saw* something amiss. Her vision was partially dazzled by the white light of the television screen but she could have sworn that at one stage a shadow passed behind the set – a dark but definite shadow. Of course, she told herself, she must be imagining things, and resolutely forced her gaze back to the wilder but somehow more reassuring adventures on the screen. But then, a few moments later, she could have sworn that once again there was a vague, shadowy movement.

By the time Angela had plucked up courage to go and switch on the dimmed lights and really look around there was, of course, nothing to be seen. If she had jumped up and flicked on the lights the very moment after the initial incident – then what would she have seen? She had no idea, no idea at all. She could only surmise with some apprehension, but also a certain perverse curiosity.

When she went to bed that night Angela Prendergast was

very careful to lock her bedroom door behind her, to fasten the window latches and draw the curtains across – and to leave a light blazing all night. That way she felt she could relax and enjoy a good night's sleep – which in fact was precisely what she did. In the morning she awoke, refreshed, and after waiting the usual interval for the fire to take the chill off the cold air, jumped out of bed and performed her usual ablutions ... in the middle of which, like a strange whisper of nostalgia, there drifted across the room that same haunting sound of a sigh.

This time, truth to be told, Angela was not quite as disturbed as on the first occasion. After all, familiarity begins to breed – well, a kind of familiarity. She was alarmed, it is true, and quickly protected herself from prying eyes – but she hardly bothered to look for any possible intruders. No, the main point now to be considered was not whether there was anyone about – but just what or who? Animal, vegetable, mineral – or human? Angela could not yet be quite sure, though she had a pretty shrewd idea.

Of course, Angela spent the rest of the morning telling herself, it was quite ridiculous. If there really was an intruder then it was her duty to ring up the police at once. But then, she managed to convince herself without much difficulty, the police would probably think she was just an hysterical woman, imagining things.

Far from imagining things, Angela was beginning to recognise with some satisfaction that she was simply observing realities. Over the next few days it became increasingly obvious that she was, mysteriously, not alone in the house any longer. Someone, something – no, she preferred to think of the intruder as someone – was there in the background, hovering watchfully, patiently waiting ...

The intriguing thing (to her as much as it would have been to any more detached observer) was that Angela did not feel afraid. Perhaps this had something to do with the quality of that first tremulous sigh which she had caught on the passing wind. There had been about it some kind of desolation, an echo of loneliness, to match her own. Yes, that was it. Somehow she felt sure that whoever it was that had come to haunt her with his presence – and of course, being a spinster, it never occurred to her that it was other than a member of the opposite sex – was someone perhaps rather like herself, a little lost, unsure and uncertain, and even shy.

Yet, she could not help noticing, he had come *here*, into her house. Why? What could possibly draw someone in this fashion, encouraging them to commit a crime like breaking in and trespassing? Why – Angela found herself blushing suddenly – there could only be one answer. Herself. Yes, herself indeed.

The strange thing was that from the moment she realised she was actively wanted and needed by someone Angela Prendergast became a changed woman. Like some plant that had too long been deprived of sunshine and water, suddenly she seemed visibly to bloom. It is true she took to spending long periods at her dressing table, brushing her long dark hair, rubbing oil into her face, trying on some glittering earrings and necklaces left by her mother – all the same, in the process her eyes seemed to shine more brightly, her hair to gleam more warmly, her skin to acquire a new kind of creaminess.

It wasn't long before people in the village began to notice the change. Several of them commented upon it among themselves, while one or two, like Mr Simmons, the new curate, and Mr Holman, the widowed chemist, felt emboldened to approach Miss Prendergast in person. It was a lovely morning, was it not? Was there anything Miss Prendergast needed? It must be rather difficult for a young lady like her to manage on her own. Perhaps –

To all of which Miss Angela Prendergast replied with a sweet smile and a regretful negative nod of the head. She appreciated this new-found interest in her well-being, but really what was the point? By now time had elapsed – several days in fact – and yet every day there had been some new sign, some further indication of that secret, now rather heartening presence. And indeed, only the day before Angela had conducted the final, conclusive test. Following an imaginative hunch she had carefully left a plateful of food on the dining room table before going to bed ... In the morning, when she came down, the plate was empty.

This had not only confirmed all Angela's half-formed suspicions, but also her resolve. That very same morning she had travelled over to the nearest market town on a shopping spree, returning by taxi laden with all manner of exciting and exotic cardboard boxes which, on her return, she carried up to her bedroom.

That evening Angela Prendergast had been especially meticulous about her preparations. First she had spent a long time in her bedroom making up her face, rouging her soft cheeks just a little, touching her anticipatory lips with a modern pale lipstick, applying just a daring dash of eye-black. Next, rigged out in a rather stunningly smart green flimsy dress she had picked up at a fashionable store, she had gone downstairs to enjoy a quiet but delectable supper. She had partaken of the meal earlier than usual that evening because she had already made certain momentous decisions in her mind, and one of them, indeed the chief, was to retire to bed early that night. But before going to bed Angela was careful to lay another place at the table, leaving a tasty, succulent cold dish, followed by fresh fruit salad and cream. Then just before going upstairs she scribbled a few significant words on a white card, signed her name with a flourish, and left the card propped up against a glass of rich red wine.

Once in her bedroom Angela Prendergast behaved in a manner somewhat different than usual. For one thing, she did not make any attempt to lock the door. For another, she was strangely casual in the manner in which she divested herself of her clothes, dropping them off one by one as she moved restlessly about the room. When finally she was completely undressed she picked up the last of her cardboard boxes and extracted from it the saucy nightdress she had bought for herself – black and frilly and rather transparent. For a while she stood in front of the mirror, clutching the nightie against her white, ample bosom and looking, indeed, the very epitome of the sort of woman who most enjoyed the pleasures of life, to the eternal vexation of their more prim sisters.

Then, with a curious gurgle of mischievous laughter, Angela quickly donned her new nightie and got into bed. Where she sat, comfortable and relaxed, occasionally brushing the long tresses of her long luxuriant hair, until the clock at her bedside rang a certain appointed hour. With a sudden quite ravishing smile she turned her head expectantly.

And slowly the bedroom door began to open ...

IX

All in the Game

May and Johnny Morgan were somewhat unique among their large circle of friends. Because May worked as a fashion designer and her husband was in advertising, their society tended to come from these worlds, in which there is a notoriously high rate of marital unhappiness. What was unusual about May and Johnny was that in more than a decade of marriage they had never even contemplated divorce and the fact was that *their* marital unhappiness rated nothing beyond an occasional disagreement such as over the boarding school progress of their two charming young sons, or perhaps about which television programme should be turned on or off – that sort of thing.

May was a tall and statuesque blonde in her mid-thirties, the sort of woman who could still make men's heads turn ... Johnny, a few years older, had one of those leonine faces with a thick crinkly crown of hair whose touches of grey were somehow an added attraction. Together they made an exceedingly handsome couple and living as they did in a handsome and comfortable flat in a flourishing South Cornish seaside resort – well, they were regarded by many people with very considerable admiration.

One morning, lying in the peace of their large and comfortable bed – it was not actually just any morning, but the morning of their thirteenth wedding day anniversary and as ever, ignoring the omens, Johnny had booked a table for dinner at their favourite Italian restaurant – May and Johnny came to a strange yet surprisingly unanimous conclusion. Though their bodies were still as warm and alive as when they had first met, though their love-making, if slightly less passionate, was just as enjoyable, though they never tired of each other's company, though there was almost nothing they could really find to complain about in their marriage – wasn't it perhaps about time they began to disagree just a little?

'I don't mean anything serious,' said May.

'No, of course not.' Johnny looked at her affectionately. 'I mean, can you imagine us having a really serious row?' He paused and added with emphasis, 'Not like the Browns, for instance.'

'Oh, the Browns!' exclaimed May, referring to a couple who tended to dominate most parties recently by enacting furious (and often physical) quarrels in public. 'The way they go on! Why, the other night he actually gave her a black eye.'

'Yes, I saw that. And she scratched his face – there was blood everywhere.'

'It was quite disgusting.' May paused, and shifted into a more comfortable position. 'All the same, in a way you must admit there was a certain –'

'Excitement?'

'No, silly. I didn't mean so much the act itself. You know, anyway, I can't bear violence of any kind.'

Johnny prodded her gently and grinned.

'Shall we say, almost any kind?'

May smiled rather fondly, and gave him a brief caress.

'Well, anyway, what I'm trying to say is –'

'You're fed up?'

'No, of course not.'

'Discontented?'

'No.'

'Well, then –?'

Johnny looked genuinely puzzled. He lay back with his hands behind his head and stared up at the brocaded ceiling.

'Let's try and analyse things, shall we? You and I have been

156

married thirteen years to the day. We seem to have been exceedingly happy. All our friends appear to regard us as an ideal couple. We have two delightful children. As far as I know, they have no complaints. As far as I know, we have no complaints. As far as I know –'

He stopped suddenly and looked sharply at May. For some reason, no doubt because of their instinctive closeness, they both thought of the answer at the same time. Johnny put it into words.

'We're just a teeny bit bored?'

'Exactly. Not so much with each other, just with life. And what I'm trying to say,' went on May, warming to her theme so that she half sat up in bed exposing a pleasing amount of bare shoulder and bosom which Johnny absentmindedly began to stroke, 'is that maybe, without going as far as the Browns, of course, we might manage to liven things up a bit.'

There was a momentary silence, while Johnny went on absentmindedly stroking his wife's unresponsive bosom.

'Well?' said May, still immersed in her new idea. 'What do you think?'

It was impossible for Johnny not to agree, not from any ulterior motive, but simply because he and May were so much in tune that they tended to think along the same lines almost automatically. He could quite see that there was a lot to be said for the idea. It would, in the first place, provide something new, a kind of challenge. It would most certainly intrigue all their friends, which should be rather amusing. And then, too, there was, it had to be admitted, something faintly erotic about the very conception.

'I don't mean that we need have any big rows or fights or anything like that,' said May warningly.

'No, of course not, I quite appreciate that. Just a few minor tiffs and arguments, eh?'

'Yes.' May bit her underlip as she began mapping out her plan of campaign. 'We'd have to begin quietly. A rather angry exchange perhaps ... and then some sort of scene, something more dramatic.'

157

'Not *too* dramatic.'

They were both anxious not to overstep the mark in any way.

'Oh, no.' May bit her lip again and resumed her planning. 'Now then, I wonder ...'

Johnny lay back in bed and stared at the ceiling. Soon they would have to be stirring: he had to get ready for his daily journey to the advertising agency, May to prepare for work in her converted studio at the end of the flat. Soon the inevitable pattern of their daily life would be set into motion, though of course it would have a break that evening with their cosy and intimate and probably rather sentimental dinner at the trattoria. Well, that would be nice, something to look forward to ... He was really very fond of his wife, he seldom ceased to marvel at their long love affair. Stirred by the thought, he turned and kissed May gently.

'Mmmmmh,' said May, her mind still rather far away. Then, taking the kiss as a sign that the day's events must be faced, she threw off the bedclothes and stood up, her familiar statuesque self.

'You know,' said May to Johnny, with a pleasant, conspiratorial smile, 'I think it's all going to be a bit of a lark.'

They began their new policy that evening at the trattoria. If they had been alone, as indeed they had intended, probably they would have left things, in view of the occasion. But some friends happened to come in later on and Johnny felt they ought at least to be invited to join in a celebratory drink. May and Johnny had by that time consumed nearly two bottles of champagne and so, in a generous mood, Johnny ordered another bottle. Soon they and their friends were busily toasting one another ... and before long the third bottle was empty. At once Johnny called out for another bottle.

'Johnny!' exclaimed May, in a strange, reproving voice that surprised not only Johnny, but even more their friends, unused as they were to any kind of disharmony between the Morgans.

'What is it, darling?' said Johnny, in all innocence.

'Really, Johnny – that's *four* bottles. I mean well – I do think its too bad of you.'

May's voice was still painfully tinted with that unfamiliar hard edge: but at the same time somehow her eyes managed to signal their urgent message through to her momentarily bewildered husband – *remember, we agreed, the game!*

'Oh, ah, yes,' said Johnny. Then pulling himself together he adopted a much sterner tone: 'Oh, for God's sake, May, stop being such a wet blanket. Just because we've been married thirteen years it doesn't give you the right to start nagging. Just shut up and drink your champagne!'

There was a curious, indeed almost stunned silence, until the waiter brought the extra bottle. Glasses were hurriedly filled and toasts frantically exchanged, but there was suddenly a flatness about everything, perhaps even the champagne. As soon as they decently could May and Johnny's friends gathered their things and went off somewhere.

When they had gone May sat back and let out peal after peal of what sounded to Johnny rather unreal laughter.

'Did you see their faces? Oh, goodness – did you see?'

'Yes, they looked pretty sick. I can just imagine what they're saying.'

'But of course – that's the whole idea.'

May leaned forward and put an utterly friendly hand upon Johnny's. Seeing the slightly disconsolate expression lingering on his handsome face she gave his hand a squeeze.

'Don't you understand? This is just what we decided to do – stir things up a little. Give them something to gossip about. You *know*.'

Johnny nodded, just a trifle dubiously. He took another swig at the champagne and began to cheer up.

'Yes, I do see. You're quite right, of course.'

'Of course I am,' declared May, confident from the certainty of her many glasses of champagne. 'Just you wait and see – the fun is just beginning.'

As it happened May's little strategy at the trattoria made an excellent and most successful opening move in the game.

Word spread like wildfire among their friends and the next time they were invited to a party they were watched in positively hawklike fashion for some further slip-ups. Normally neither May nor Johnny would have noticed such attention, but now somehow the knowledge made them both a trifle uncomfortable, and even edgy: to cover this discomfiture they both drank rather more than usual. After a while, wishing to demonstrate to May that he was fully able to participate in the new game on equal terms, Johnny made some rather caustic remarks about one of his wife's latest fashion designs, to a group with whom he was talking. The remarks were not terribly wounding but Johnny's anxiety to play the game fully resulted in his voice seeming to ring out all over the room. Once again, as in the restaurant, there was a strange hush ... and meaningful glances were exchanged, before in the end, humanely, other topics of conversation were reluctantly resumed.

Quite early for them May and Johnny collected their coats and said a rather brusque farewell to their hosts, and departed into the night.

'Well,' said Johnny, as they waited outside for a taxi. 'Guess what they're talking about up there, eh?'

'Us,' said May rather coldly, and she said nothing more for the whole of the taxi journey back, or indeed for the rest of that night.

In the morning, when they both felt a little better, though somewhat hangovery, she said as casually as possible to Johnny, while he was shaving.

'Did you *really* mean what you said about my new design?'

'Blast!' exclaimed Johnny. 'Now look what you've done, you've made me go and cut myself. Look, I'm *bleeding*!'

He picked up a piece of tissue and dabbed furiously at the cut.

'No, of course I didn't mean it,' he said at last; but perhaps a shade late in the day.

May had what might be called her own back at dinner some nights later. It was at the house of two of their oldest friends, and this confinement seemed to throw an enormous spotlight upon the barbed, delicate and somewhat contemptuous way in which May proceeded to analyse a current advertisement in the day's newspaper, which all knew to be Johnny's total responsibility.

'Just one of your off-moments I expect, dear,' she finished sweetly.

'Oh, is that so?' said Johnny icily. 'Is that so, indeed?'

The dinner party continued, conversation hurriedly switched to other spheres, but the spark had gone out of things. Even the food, much to the hostess's fury, seemed curiously tasteless, so that she was led to blame her culinary disappointment upon May and Johnny's childish behaviour. What she and her husband had to say, when their visitors were gone, is best not repeated.

'That advertisement of mine,' said Johnny carefully the next morning, while the two of them still lay in a reasonable state of composed contentment. 'You were a bit scathing about it, weren't you?'

'Was I?' said May uneasily. She had rather forgotten the incident and would certainly have preferred to have left it at that.

'Yes, you were.'

'Oh, don't be silly. You're imagining things.'

May stirred restlessly.

'What's the time? We ought to be getting up soon.'

'Well?' said Johnny persistently.

'Well, what?'

'Well, did you *really* mean what you said about that advertisement?'

'Oh, Johnny!' Seeking solace in action, May got out of bed and began dressing quickly. 'For goodness' sake, do remember – we agreed on all this. It's just a game.'

Johnny lay back and stared unhappily up at the ceiling..

'Mmmmhhh,' he said at last. 'I suppose so.'

It was surprising, they both discovered, how comparatively easy it was to find weapons of attack – how many vulnerable

161

spots lay exposed. After May's designs, there was May's cooking – not one of her best attributes. After Johnny's advertising techniques, there was Johnny's punctuality, an abysmal failing. There was May's extravagance, May's sentimentality, May's laziness – even, on one occasion when Johnny felt especially mean, May's narcissism. Contrariwise, there was Johnny's intellectual arrogance, Johnny's male conceit, Johnny's forgetfulness – and, when in turn May sought more ammunition, Johnny's lack of loyalty.

For some reason, whereas May remained comparatively unmoved about her narcissism (since she was perfectly prepared to admit it existed) Johnny appeared considerably put out about the imputation of disloyalty.

'When have I ever been disloyal? Come on, now, when? How can you possibly say a thing like that. And in front of our friends, too.'

It being the next morning, and tempers presumably all calm again, May spoke pacifyingly:

'Oh, do stop going on so. You know perfectly well it's just a game.'

And feeling rather pleased with herself, for at the previous evening's engagement several men had extravagantly complimented her on her attractive appearance (a fact which Johnny had not failed to observe) May began humming a familiar tune.

'It's all in the game ...'

'Well,' said Johnny angrily, coming over to the dressing table where May sat brushing her hair and admiring her face in the mirror, 'it's not all in the game to me!'

And he slapped her hard across the cheek, leaving a large red weal, before marching out of the room.

Soon matters developed to the point where friends of May and Johnny began holding secret conferences and worriedly discussing what might be done. At various times May was taken aside, or Johnny was led away to a corner, and there were long, earnest discussions and appeals to reason. Since usually, after they had recovered from any momentary quarrel, May and Johnny were still pretending to one another that they were still playing a game, they were able to extract a certain amount of rueful humour from these earnest approaches. At the same time they agreed (rather readily as it happened, if a trifle hopefully) that it would be politic to give the impression of being suitably influenced by these well-meant approaches. Consequently their friends began to feel quite encouraged.

'Ah, yes, things are going much better now, I think you'll find.'

'Of course, I never did believe it was anything serious. I mean, May and Johnny, why they're so ideally suited.'

'It's all blowing over, just a storm in a teacup.'

Unfortunately at the very next party May chose to flirt ostentatiously with a complete stranger who did not really appreciate she was married nor indeed, unfortunately for his wellbeing, that her seething husband was also present. The scene that followed was, as someone put it, rather like something out of a Scott Fitzgerald novel, only worse. Johnny knocked a tooth out of the stranger's mouth, and in return suffered a bloody nose. May, weeping copiously, had to be put to bed in the spare bedroom.

When Johnny came home from work the next evening he bore with him a large bunch of flowers as a peace offering. Unfortunately their glossy effect was dimmed as May was not there, and did not return until nearly midnight. She had, in fact, simply gone to a cinema as she felt too nervous, after what had happened, to face the evening encounter with Johnny. When she did finally return, her husband – whether playing the game or not it was difficult to tell, but somehow she rather had her doubts – at once accused her of having been out with her 'friend' of the previous evening.

'How utterly absurd! How perfectly childish!' said May, and quite a few other, more pungent remarks. Johnny replied in kind. In the end they went to their bedroom in silence and lay as far apart as was possible in a bed really designed, and for some thirteen years regularly utilised, as a true marital couch.

After that the game might be said to have progressed, at a positively alarming rate, towards set and match. At parties the Browns were no longer the centre of attraction indeed they became positive nonentities. From the moment they entered the room, ostentatiously together and yet equally obviously apart, it was now the Morgans who claimed general attention. It was possibly true even at that late stage that some spirit of the game lingered: that is to say, when May deliberately blew a cloud of smoke into Johnny's eyes making him cough and splutter in the middle of an important conversation – or when Johnny tipped a glass of red wine down the front of May's latest rather provocative almost-see-through outfit – when these things happened each perhaps experienced a certain amount of enjoyment in the act, even the possible violence after the act. There is always an actor's ego lurking in us all ... indeed there were still odd occasions, back home going to bed after some party, when – forgetting for a moment the real state of the nation – May or Johnny would suddenly turn and remark, 'I say, did you see the look on their faces? Wasn't it marvellous! You know, when I threw that –'

And then the remark would fade away uneasily as it became rather obvious that the recipient of the thrown object, and of most of the ridicule, was not in the least amused.

It went on for a little while yet, the game. For one thing there were the school holidays to be survived, the children home and appearances to be kept up. In a wild, almost insane burst of forced jollity they took the boys with them on a series of outings, to cinemas and to the theatre and various other public places where conventional restrictions would ensure things being kept on a safe level.

Only in the silent privacy of the bedroom – joint occupation of which had been impelled by consideration of their sons' feelings – were things allowed to find their natural level.

'You know I had no idea,' said Johnny pleasantly, 'what an

utter bitch you could be.'

May lay icy and cold in her well-defined part of the bed.

'Thanks for the compliment. But then you always were one for the graceful word – I don't think!'

The night hung heavy and sleepless. It usually did, once they embarked on the exchange of such pleasantries. Neither of them could bear to give the other the last word, that was the trouble. In a way it was a dangerous extension of the game, if such a word could be loosely used, to which they became now increasingly devoted ... The fact was that they now found they got a very real pleasure out of seeking some ultimate rapier thrust, some brilliant piece of repartee, some really devastating witticism which might extinguish the enemy. Unfortunately they discovered in battle, as they had found in the bygone days of peace, that each was a complete foil for the other, and usually they drifted drowsily and grumblingly into sleep.

Sometimes in the mornings, especially after the children had returned to boarding school (feeling extremely uneasy about their parents) May and Johnny would attempt to resume the night's battles. But generally they were in too much of a hurry to be off and away: Johnny to reach the comfort of his office, where he could embark on a series of by now somewhat boring confidences to his colleagues about his misunderstanding wife ... May to settle down at the phone and ring up a few friends to launch into her own equally tedious revelations.

'Those Morgans ... They really are becoming *impossible.*'

'Too true. Do you know, I had May on the phone today for nearly an hour!'

'Can't you do something, Gerald? You're one of Johnny's oldest friends.'

'I've tried, I really have.'

'What about you, Mary? You and May have known each other years.'

'Do you know, it's funny, but I feel as if I hardly know her at all now.'

'Well, *something's* got to be done. They'll tear each other to pieces.'

Armed by that self-protective intuition that lies within us all May and Johnny did not tear each other to pieces, though sometimes, undoubtedly, they came near to doing so. Or at least, they *appeared* to do so. Not only did their friends continue to find their scenes and quarrels still somehow incredible – so, often, did May and Johnny. Sometimes there were moments when, contemplating each other in a state of amazement at their situation, perhaps a gesture a word even, might have put everything right. Alas it was not to be: they seemed both to have succumbed to the ritual of perpetual warfare, unable to relinquish the new drug. After a somewhat turbulent while they finally agreed, in a moment of calm, that it might be wisest to separate. Divorce was an idea sometimes referred to, but for the time being allowed to lie fallow. May went on living in the flat, and Johnny moved into a bed sitter. Official letters were composed in consultation and sent to the children: there was much talk of all being together at holiday times, remaining good friends and so on. Subsequently, unofficial letters were surreptitiously sent which confused the children greatly, so that they wrote worriedly and at random to both parents, with the result that the later subterfuges were exposed.

'I just rang up,' said Johnny coldly on the phone one day, 'to express my abhorrence of the cowardly way you went behind my back and wrote to the children.'

'Unfortunately for your mock righteousness I have only this morning received a communication from the children which makes it quite plain that you too ...'

The telephones clicked firmly back on to their hooks: and that, for nearly a year – apart from a few false holiday encounters – was that. Johnny plunged into his work, staying late at the office, creating endless new ideas for brilliant new campaigns, earning more and more money, as well as the praise of colleagues – and remaining thoroughly miserable in his bachelor rooms, unable even to summon up interest in having an affair with several women who would have been only too willing. May for her part, with more time on her hands than ever before, also sought solace in work: her designs positively spermed out by the dozen, inspired by a new cynicism admirably suited to the current mode. She, too, made a lot more money, most of which she spent, almost perversely, improving the appearance of the flat. Sometimes she entertained friends, but always she was glad to see them go, and to throw herself exhausted on the large and now rather lonely bed. Usually she took the transistor radio set up to bed at night and let the music lull her to sleep. One night it suddenly blared out a familiar tune, and the smooth, treacly voice of Billy Eckstine assured her it was all in the game. May abruptly switched off the radio, and turned her head to the pillow and began crying.

Johnny did not cry, because men are not supposed to cry: but he felt an increasing sense of emptiness in his life as the long months went by, and came to feel sick to death of advertising and copywriting and campaigns and – well, everything. He began staying away from the office; and worse, taking to the bottle. Not really what might be called alcoholism, but a fondness for the oblivions of drink that worried his friends, just as May's state of growing indifference was beginning to worry her friends. They no longer had the same friends, of course, as 'mutuals' had had to make their choice and settle for one side or the other, but there was no doubt a certain amount of unofficial fraternisation ... as a result of which little items of news began to filter through to the opposing camps. May heard that Johnny was drinking himself to death – being a narcissist she naturally assumed it was over her. Johnny heard that May was wasting away, positively wraith-like (fortunately this was something of an overstatement) – being a realist he appreciated that this was for love of him. These things in themselves were not enough to achieve any major change in the general situation but they remained like the proverbial ripples in the pool, that went on rippling, fed as they were by a new discreet stone being

167

dropped into the water every now and then. Johnny was not only drinking more, he hardly ever stopped, he looked quite ghastly. May spent most of the day sitting around crying, her eyes were red-rimmed from weeping. Johnny would soon be getting the sack from the advertising agency if he didn't buck up. May had lost quite a lot of important orders, she just didn't seem to have the same spark. And so on and so on.

A year had passed to the day when Johnny found himself wandering rather aimlessly down one of those cafe-strewn, car-lined gaily lit streets and turned, almost without thinking, into the familiar entrance of the small Italian trattoria. It was a long time, he reflected, since he had been in that particular restaurant, indeed he could hardly bear to contemplate the memories that came floating back. How long in fact? His mind, a little fuddled from an earlier drinking session, took quite a while to register the extraordinary fact that the time was exactly a year, and that today was his wedding anniversary, immediately overcome at the mournful thought he would have risen to leave, but by then a waiter had come forward confidently to take his order ... and since it was a strange waiter, and not one who would have known him from the past, and he felt so utterly miserable, anyway, Johnny subsided into a window seat and ordered a bottle of Chianti and, without much interest, some food.

It was at about this moment that a woman called Amy walked down that particular street and past that particular Italian trattoria and, looking casually in the window, recognised Johnny. The woman called Amy has no further place or importance in this story except that she happened to be a very old friend of both May and Johnny; unlike many others, a real, true friend; and, what is more, providentially, a woman of some imagination. She could not positively have sworn that Johnny was sitting *crying* at the table where she knew once a year he and May always had their anniversary dinner but by the time, breathless, she had reached a telephone box and rung May, she was absolutely certain. 'Weeping into his wine glass, my dear, weeping ... ' was how she put it with considerable and commendable poetic licence. She had intended to make some rather obvious suggestion about May getting a taxi but before she could say anything further the phone went dead as May set off immediately on that very quest. Wearing a large and deserved halo, Amy walked away into her own life again.

Johnny had finished toying with his food and drunk most of the Chianti and was almost on the point of leaving when the taxi drew up with a slight screech of brakes, and the apparition appeared in the doorway. Every other time Johnny had seen May in that particular setting she had always been dolled up: shimmering evening dress, long ear-rings, a smart new coiffure. Tonight, having forgotten all else in the urgency of the moment, she still wore a pair of slacks and a plain turquoise jersey – indeed in some restaurants might have been barred.

Fortunately the trattoria was not that sort of restaurant. It was the sort of place that could take in its stride a couple greeting each other like long lost souls, as if they had not seen each other for at least a hundred years. Politely the waiters kept out of the way as May stood for a time rooted in the middle of the corridor between the tables, until at last, at a mute gesture from an overwhelmed Johnny, she took the seat opposite him. Johnny would never know – May would soon forget – the brief but necessary part played in the story by Amy. Soon – see, already it was happening as one hand crept out tentatively to clasp the other – they would remember only the wonderful and indeed stupendous fact that on this, their wedding anniversary, they had both chosen to return to the scene of so much happiness. It seemed almost too true to be good.

At a signal from the manager the waiter bent forward unobtrusively.

'Some more wine, signor?'

Johnny stared into May's eyes. May stared back. The waiter coughed, understanding these situations, and waited.

'No,' said Johnny at last. 'No more wine.' He smiled a

brilliant smile that to May was like the sun itself, and even to the waiter a most welcome sight, for he recognised from long experience the smile of a man in love, who would therefore be bound to leave an exceedingly handsome tip.

'We will have,' said Johnny with enormous bonhomie, 'a bottle of champagne.'

'Yes,' said May, a little tremulously. 'We have something to celebrate.'

The waiter bowed. It was a pleasure to serve such people. He went off to prepare with all due ceremony a bottle of champagne worthy of the occasion.

As for May and Johnny, they could hardly find words to say. They didn't really need to, after all. Instead, they just sat there holding hands, tightly, even a little desperately, as if they would never, never let go again. And the game began all over again – only this time, fortunately, the right way round.

A few days later May and Johnny's two sons sat under a tree in their school playground reading a letter.

'It's from Dad and Mum.'

'What does it say?'

'They're back together again.'

'Well, honestly.'

The boys looked at one another and sniffed. *Parents.*

Then they went off to play football.

X

The Way of the Healer

Manson was a healer – a dark, quiet middle-aged man who had dedicated most of his life to fulfilling the strange powers of cure and re-creation contained in his big thick-veined hands. He had long, soft-tipped fingers that pressed deep into resistent flesh, probing among swollen tissues and disturbed ligaments, persuasively moulding and manipulating them back into their functional patterns. Gently and unhurriedly, like the coming and going of the seasons, Manson's hands brought an end to pain and kindled new flows of life. They were the instruments of his genius: behind lay concentrated physical energy, a swift and decisive mind, the flame of faith.

Manson had a consulting office with windows looking out on to colourful flowerbeds and neat-cut lawns. Here, in a small, cream-walled treatment room, he saw his patients. They came in a steady stream; ten, twelve, sometimes more, every day; and while they were with him he gave himself wholly to their problems, their broken limbs, tired hearts, their weary maladjustments. Lying so utterly defenceless on the massage table they appeared to him very much like children, pathetic and trusting, and he approached them as a kind father, acutely aware of his responsibilities. They came to him from different worlds, but in his treatment room they became for him a fusion of all their worlds. When he put his hands gently upon their bodies he felt that he was touching the body of all suffering humanity, and if he was able to bring

171

only the slightest measure of relief he was filled with a great sense of joy. It did not seem to him to matter much who they were or what they were: they were merely there to be helped and comforted. So he gave himself up fervently to that task – absorbed in his work and yet at the same time remaining detached in himself. Until, unsuspectingly, he received a new patient.

She came to him one delicate April morning. She was a tall, graceful woman in her early thirties, wearing neatly tailored clothes that still could not hide the swift, suggestive lines of her body. She walked into the treatment room with the easy confidence of a woman supremely in possession of herself, and there was about her an intense, almost animal-like vibration of aliveness. When she sat facing Manson, the sunlight slanting across a mass of reddish-brown hair and catching the silver sheen of her stockings, he suddenly realized that she must be the most beautiful woman he could remember seeing there. And she exhibited her knowledge of this fact with an almost insolent casualness.

He watched her settle into the chair, stretching herself in a lazy but controlled movement.

'I shouldn't have thought there was anything radically wrong with you,' he commented dryly, fingering a pencil and a blank diagnosis chart. He felt a vague irritation at her presence, as if pricked by some presentiment.

He asked the usual questions. She answered him directly, her voice lowered, rather husky. She was a dancer – at first ballet, now a specialty dancer. Her dances demanded concentration and suppleness. Lately her body had felt tired; it seemed to have lost its natural rhythm. She wanted someone to bring back the rhythm, the flow of life.

'I'll see what I can do,' he said. But he was surprised with himself for the words. He knew he would normally refuse such requests in favour of more serious cases.

While she undressed behind a curtain he stood staring out of the window; but somehow he could not prevent himself hearing the leisurely rustle of her movements. When she was

172

lying face downwards on the bench he came from behind and
laid his fingers around the nape of her neck, pushing aside the
straggly clusters of curls. Then, delicately, he ran his hands
down the back, fanning the fingers outwards along the
rippling waves of muscle and flesh. Expertly he traced the
sensitive tone and resilience. Here and there he fashioned out
tiny symptoms of strain and tiredness. In truth, the back was
in better condition than in the case of many patients he had
sent away pronounced healthy. Still, he thought, justifying
himself, she is different. As a dancer her body must be more
highly tuned ... He began moving his hands up and down the
white curve of the back, slipping into a slow flowing
movement, until it was difficult to distinguish his hands from
the flesh, and they were all merged into a whole, like waves in
the sea. He prepared to become absorbed in his work,
directing his fingers in their endless probing; a touch here, a
gentle adjustment there, deep under the cloak of whiteness ...
It was good to feel through the tips of his fingers the healing
and regeneration of a human body, to feel the blood racing
and surging. It was always a pleasure to him, this moment
when he felt himself welded to the patient, willing a part of his
own strength into the other. There was no real reason why this
should be any other than the mechanical process that he had
followed on hundreds of previous occasions. Yet he became
conscious, almost against his will, of some extra sensation
conveyed into his hands. It was almost as if, despite his
conscious attempt to automatize himself, a perverse will outside
himself was forcing this further sensory feeling upon him. He
glanced at the tousled hair, splashed about like a red mist. He
wondered whether her eyes were closed; or perhaps round and
open? Uneasily, he resumed the massage. Despite himself he
found his eyes falling on the firm outline of the body. For it
was a beautiful body. He could not only see its beauty against
the austere background of the massaging table – he could feel
it in his hands. There was something alive about the beauty
that transmitted into the tips of his fingers. He felt his mind
drift away, thinking in a way that had never before occurred to

him, about other bodies that had lain there. Thick bodies, fat bodies, lumpy bodies, diseased and decaying bodies, broken and shattered bodies. He found himself thinking that it was like feeling fresh water in his face to feel in his hands the cool whiteness of a beautiful body.

He worked on steadily moulding the flesh as if he were creating a beautiful carving or etching. When at last he stopped, it was as if he came out of a dream. His hands, conscious of their tiredness, dropped heavily against the sides of his white coat. Looking down at the back, now flushed a delicate pink from the manipulation, he felt a strange tingle in his fingers – an irresistible desire to rejoin them to the back.

'I think that should be sufficient,' he said gruffly. 'There are no indications of adhesions, just a little strain and overwork.' He hesitated. Really he was not justified in continuing with a case of this nature. He tried to think of other patients he ought to be seeing. They remained beyond his reach, conveniently in shadow.

As he stood thinking the red hair jerked and she swung upright. She stretched her arms wide, a gesture of sheer physical contentment. Like an animal, he thought, oddly.

'I feel marvellous,' she said. She half-draped a dressing-gown over her shoulders. Drawn irresistibly his eyes met hers, fell, and traced the upward swell of a breast. He looked away quickly. It was ridiculous, she was merely a patient, another patient. Yet his irritation was tinged with a perverse sense of delight to think that it was his hands that could bring the life pulsating again through her body, could renew its elixir.

When she was dressing behind the curtain she called out: 'Perhaps you would be good enough to book me for another appointment?'

Some underlying implication of insolence made him flush, almost goaded him into an angry reply.

'Really,' he began, 'do you think it's necessary?'

He heard her laugh. The echo mocked him.

'Oh, but I think it's very necessary,' she said.

He turned round, uncertainly. She came out from behind

the curtain. She was once again suave, sleekly dressed, but he found himself seeking her as she had lain on the table and all the hot words sank away from him.

'Don't you?' she said directly.

'Yes,' he said. 'Yes, by all means ...'

It began thus simply. By all the professional sense ingrained into him, Manson felt that he was not justified in accepting her as a patient. Yet something beyond that made it impossible for him to refuse. She came again three days after the first appointment, and after that she came several times a week.

At first he held himself taut, erecting a wall of defence around him, but the result was to leave him nervous and irritable, unable to concentrate on his other work. Then, perhaps foolishly, he went to see her dance. He seldom went to the theatre – he was usually too tired anyway – but he felt he could not churlishly refuse her offer of a seat. The moment she appeared on the stage he felt himself drawn up out of the darkness. She had just one dance, but it was an extraordinarily long one that obviously left her exhausted. It was symbolic, the dance of the native girl ordained to be sacrificed to the Gods. It began slowly, almost sedately, then by a subtle swaying of her body she conveyed a sense of urgency and the tempo mounted, while other dancers twisted around in a menacing circle. Thereafter, at each leap of the music, at each beat of the drum, the spotlighted dancer swayed faster and faster, spinning her body into wild sensuous shapes. The face was held in a look of savage disdain, but behind this mask the eyes burned bright and frightening. Somehow Manson could not resist the feeling that they burned at him, taunting him. He sat there held to the seat, as the dance writhed to a crescendo, and the white, familiar body prostrated itself in exhaustion before the gaudy pedestal of an artificial god. Then he got up and left the theatre.

The next time she visited him he felt a new tension between them. When she asked him if he enjoyed the dance and he

175

said, but curtly, that he had, he felt her eyes upon him. In their shadowy depths he read knowledge of what he had felt, and he knew that a strange triumph lay in that knowledge. Now he began to feel himself being drawn under her power. It was true that instinct prompted him to proceed through the mechanical routine, the sweep of his fingers up and down the back, the widening outwards, the soft curving and folding of the flesh – it was true that the treatment was precisely the same as he would apply to another patient. But now, unmistakably, he felt, through the tips of his fingers, his awareness of her growing into a living thing. Now as she lay there, try as he would, he could not prevent the image arising before his mind of her movements in the dance, the swaying of a thigh, the curve of a shoulder. When this happened he tightened his grip, overwhelmed by the desire to re-establish his own power, to feel her helpless before him. He wondered by what miracle he had never before had this unbearable experience of becoming aware of his patient. He tried to remember down the years – long years, nearly twenty of them since he had left his hospital job to set up on his own – but he found it quite impossible to bring other people into focus. Work had been for him everything, there had hardly been an outside world; almost all his human contacts had been patients or dispassionate medical attendants; between him and them all there had been always the small but sufficient barrier of professional detachment. Now something he could not satisfactorily define had smashed roughly across the barrier. He felt unable to prevent anything even as he sensed the futility of it all.

For now she herself, conscious of the attainment of her power, dropped the assumed conventionalities of human behaviour. Now she behaved with him like the animal she was, playing with him as a cat will play with a mouse – up to the finest limit of endurance. Now she let herself flow into his hands, until through them he felt sudden fire and passion; choosing that moment to stiffen into frigidity, sitting up and laughing into his face. Even then the battle was fought by

176

touch and through the eyes, not by words. Once she leaned across him so that her breath curled down his neck like an embrace. Or she stood so close to him that he could feel her heart beating into his own body. The contact shocked him, but he did not move. Vaguely he sensed the hidden, immeasurable stakes of the battle, and with grim perversion he fought against his surrender.

The effort and strain of this gripped him like a fever, sweeping him up to peaks of fierce ecstasy, sinking him down into seas of despondency. Nothing else held him or possessed any value for him: least of all his other patients. They became no more troublesome than shadows on the horizon.

Some final devoutness to the code of his profession prevented his giving way to the rushing desire to possess her even as she lay white and inviting in his hands. But he knew, unhappily, that the process was inevitable.

Then one day, unexpectedly, she did not arrive for her appointment. He paced irritably up and down the room, possessed by a mixture of misery and relief. At last the 'phone rang. She sounded irritated.

'Could you come round at once?' she said.

'Round?' he said stupidly. It was extraordinary, but their relationship had been so confined and focused to the tiny room, or the anonymous darkness of a theatre, that he knew hardly anything about her other life.

She made a sound of annoyance.

'Yes, if you wouldn't mind ... Someone's been hurt. An accident. I couldn't think of anyone else in the excitement.'

'Yes, of course. I'll come at once,' he said, mechanically, noting the address.

She lived on the first floor of a large block of luxury flats. When he knocked she opened the door herself. Her eyes met him with the same mocking look, but he saw that they were tinged slightly with aggravation.

'He's on the bed,' she said abruptly. 'The porters brought him up. It was very stupid – he fell out of the window. I was afraid perhaps he's broken some bones or something. Luckily this is only the first floor.'

She showed him into a big, comfortably furnished bedroom. He looked round curiously, seeing the colourful tapestries, the dainy ornaments, a frothy pile of dresses ... a photogravure memory of her whiteness. Then, crumpled across the bed, he saw the man.

He was very young, little more than a boy: young and good-looking with a dark, rather sallow face, now twisted with pain. With a detached flash-back of his mind Manson recognized him as one of the dancers in the show, one of the forlorn devotees of the native girl.

'He fell out of the window,' she repeated. She spoke crossly, as if the accident had been done specifically to annoy her. The man turned his face to one side as she spoke.

Manson bent down and began to remove the clothing, which was muddy and crumpled where it had lain on the ground. He pulled a pair of scissors out of his bag, and gently cut away the tighter portions. Then, he began running his hands up and down the body, feeling with infinite delicacy for possible fractures. He was relieved to find nothing actually broken; but there were several torn ligaments, a mass of angry red bruises.

Behind him he felt the woman relax, giving a short, almost impatient sigh. Glancing round quickly he saw her looking down at the man on the bed. He was suddenly glad that the man's eyes were turned away so that he did not see the look.

'Well,' she said, in obvious relief. 'I'll leave him to you now.' And she walked quickly out of the room.

Manson took off his coat and embarked on a more lengthy examination. It was good that he should begin the healing process at once, as far as possible. With great gentleness he began sinking his fingers into the flesh, moving them around in a circular pattern. As he worked he could sense the young man watching him, the brown, pain-flecked eyes urgent with anxiety.

At length he straightened up.

'Doctor – ?' whispered the man on the bed.

Manson bent forward. The eyes pleaded with him.

'Doctor, my legs – are they –? Will I be able to dance again?'

'Of course, of course,' he said soothingly. But it had been a near thing: it might even now take a long time. He looked across the room to the window, and tried to visualize the young man perched casually there, one moment laughing, the next –

He frowned.

'You know, you must be very careless falling out of a window,' he said.

'How did it happen?' he went on absent-mindedly, still staring across at the window.

Feeling the silence long drawn out he looked down at the bed again. He found himself staring straight into the young man's eyes. They were wide open, defenceless, and suddenly gleaming with tears. The hurt in them lurked deep down, as if it would be buried there for ever. Manson felt as if he were gazing into a mirror. He understood, suddenly, that it had not been an accident.

'It was a very foolish thing to do,' he said quietly. He ran his hand thoughtfully along the young man's legs, feeling their strength and their beauty, the rippling flesh and bone that held their capacity to create and to give meaning to life. Looking again at the wide open window he sensed, fleetingly, the impetuous despair, the agonized useless attempt to escape into the endless oblivion that lay beyond. Then he looked from the legs to his own hands, moist and familiar, 'Why,' he began, the anger surging upon him. 'Why – ' He felt a wild desire to crush the absent whiteness that had brought them both to the abyss edge. And then, a great pity sweeping everything else away, he bent down and laid a hand on the man's head.

'It's all right,' he said. 'You'll dance again, don't worry!'

He began his work there and then, and as he felt the blood flowing warmly under his fingers, the limbs easing and relaxing; as he saw in the watching brown eyes the familiar,

179

childlike, unquestioning trust; so, with a flash of joy, he saw the way clear again and knew that it lay forward, the way of the healer.

XI

In the Kingdom of the Blind

When our daughter Karenza was ten years old she went blind. A man brought her in through the garden gate after finding her groping her way along with outstretched hands down the middle of the high street in our little seaside town.

He was quite upset.

'Gave me a proper fright, the poor little mite. Didn't know what she was doing or which way to go. Besides,' he went on accusingly, 'it was causing a fair old traffic block, cars jamming the side streets and all. The policeman was in a real tizzy. But of course when he saw –'

He went away, shaking his head mournfully at the cruel injustice of the world, striking down one so young and beautiful and helpless. We were left somewhat more helpless, standing by the kitchen door and watching our eldest daughter staggering about the room.

'Karenza – for goodness sake, look out!'

Karenza rammed the kitchen table, waved her hands wildly in the air and collapsed on to a seat. With slow deliberate movements she laid her hands to rest on the table in front of her, pushing them forward as if in dumb supplication.

'Don't you understand? Have you no hearts? Just *look* at me!'

She turned towards us a face, usually ultra-familiar, now kind of screwed up in a paroxysm of indescribable anguish, a face somehow devoid of meaning as both eyes were tightly closed. She gave a sudden and heart-rending sigh.

'I'm blind ...'

My wife and I looked at one another uneasily. We were by now both used to Karenza, at least we should have been after ten years: all the same, one could never be sure.

I went and sat beside her, putting an arm round her shoulders.

'Tell us what happened? Are you sure you're not, well, imagining –?'

Karenza moaned, the anguished expression deepened and a very real tear slowly oozed out of the corner of the tightly shut eyelids and trickled down her cheeks.

'Oh – you're cruel! Cruel and heartless!'

Suddenly, with unexpected alacrity for one so helpless, she jumped to her feet and began stumbling across the kitchen towards the door.

'I *must* find help. Doctor! Hospital! Police!'

We managed to stop her before she could get involved with Mrs Moss next door and the elderly couple over the way and anyone else who might be available. I looked at my wife and shrugged.

'We'd better do something. After all, you never know. I'll ring the hospital.'

I had no idea what to say, really. It sounded somehow faintly incredible to mention casually on the phone, 'Look, I'm sorry to bother you but I think it's possible our daughter has suddenly gone blind.'

Fortunately my problems were quickly resolved. There was an eye clinic that very afternoon so we could get a taxi and go straight over. It was only after we had embarked on our dramatic journey that a tiny suspicious voice whispered at the back of my mind – it is possible, could she have *known* there was an eye clinic?

It wasn't far to the hospital, but for us the journey was a most embarrassing one. For some reason Karenza insisted on sitting in the front beside the driver, and apart from the fact that her impressively sustained poise of eyes-shut, face-anguished, hands-held-out-in-front-of-her scared the driver out of his wits – it also kindled quite a bit of attention among passers by, especially on the couple of occasions when the taxi was forced to slow down at a junction. We both cringed as we heard the pointed comments.

'Oh, look at the poor girl!'

'Fancy that, now. In agony, dear little soul.'

'Aaaaahh! Aaaaahh!' (This in response to a sudden dramatic move by Karenza, who opened her window and protruded a sightless and rather horrific face out as if blindly searching for some miracle.)

'Karenza!'

I think my wife was going to say something quite sharp and scathing, for she has a horror of public scenes ... but something about the bristling antagonism of the driver's head quelled her courage.

'You – you must be brave, Karenza,' she muttered appeasingly.

When we arrived at the hospital there was quite a performance getting Karenza out of the car, as she tripped and fell all over the place. I managed to catch her before she actually hit the ground. It was then – conscious of the youthful and very mortal young body in my arms – that I suddenly felt the beginnings of the panic I had tried to resist. Supposing she *was* blind? Supposing she *had* suddenly been struck down by some sort of terrible affliction? Supposing ...?

Breaking into a run I left my wife behind and dragged Karenza's stumbling figure after me to the reception desk.

'Quick,' I gasped. 'This girl may be seriously ill, at death's door. We must see Doctor Thingummyjig –'

'Doctor *who*?'

'You know – the eye man.'

The receptionist looked at me severely.

'Have you an appointment?'

'Appointment?' I began to rage impotently. 'Just *look* at her!'

'Help!' shrieked Karenza. 'Help!'

The receptionist stood up agitatedly.

'Now then, really, I can't allow all this noise. It'll upset – '

'Upset *who*?' It was my wife. Having apparently decided like me to give Karenza the benefit of the doubt she was ready to join doughtily in the battle. 'What about my daughter? She's seriously ill. She needs a specialist ...'

'*Now*!' she shouted at the top of her voice, startling us all and waking up several semi-comatose patients sitting around.

In the end the receptionist hurried off and after a little while we were ushered down a long corridor and into the great man's consulting room. He looked rather like most consultants: large, comfortable, calm and collected, altogether very knowing and able.

'Well, now, what appears to be the trouble?'

'I'm blind!' exclaimed Karenza. 'Blind as a bat.'

Before anyone could stop her she reeled round, held her arms out and walked straight into some elongated eye-testing contraption which crashed noisily to the ground. At the alarming sound a nurse ran in and began trying to re-erect the pieces, muttering under her breath.

'Well, now,' said the specialist again, pursing his lips. 'You'd better sit down here, young lady. And please *don't* move.'

He turned to us portentously.

'Now just briefly try and tell me –'

'Aaah! Oooh! My eyes, my eyes ... They're like balls of fire. I can feel them burning. Oh, my poor eyes ...'

'We don't know any more than you, doctor,' said my wife meekly. 'She just came home from school in this state.'

'Mmmmh.' Unwillingly, it seemed, the doctor turned back to Karenza. The first few times he put his hand out to touch her eyes she shied away, but in the end – when at a sign from him the nurse had pinned Karenza's flailing arms firmly to her side – he was able, fleetingly, to raise the eyelid on each side and peer into what horrible aspect lay hidden.

'Mmmh,' said the doctor again. He put a hand out and felt Karenza's pulse. Next he picked up a pencil and began tapping it against the gold filling of one of his teeth, eyeing his patient speculatively.

'This suddenly came on this afternoon, did it, young lady?'

'Yes, doctor. I was just walking down the street and –'

The doctor looked at us.

'Would you mind? I think it might help if I had a little chat with your daughter on my own.'

Dutifully we crept outside. We began pacing up and down the corridor, clasping and unclasping our hands, every now and then eyeing one another with tragic looks, already adjusting ourselves to our new existence as blind dog companions. I saw myself taking Karenza for her morning walk, my wife doing the afternoon one. Perhaps the other children would take their turns. And then there were meals: feeding time would become – but then, perhaps she could still manage to fend for herself? After all, there was Braille, touch typing, that sort of thing. All the same it seemed a gloomy sort of prospect.

The door opened.

'Will you come in now, please?'

The doctor, we were relieved to notice, looked once again his old, composed self. He nodded to the nurse, and turned to Karenza.

'Now, my dear, your turn to step outside for a few minutes while I have a chat with your father and mother. All right?'

Karenza nodded, and managed despite her closed eyes, to strike a dramatic pose.

'Yes, doctor. But you will tell them – *the worst* – won't you?'

When she had gone and the door was firmly shut behind her the doctor looked at us accusingly.

'Why didn't you explain about her brother?'

We looked at one another in alarm.

'What's *he* been doing?'

185

'Didn't he have his eyes tested at school recently?'

'Er, yes.'

'And wasn't he prescribed a pair of glasses?'

'Yes.'

'Which he received a week or so back and has worn ever since?'

'Well, yes, that's right.'

The doctor relaxed, looking rather smug.

'That's it, then. Your daughter's condition is merely a symptom of something else – in this case, jealousy of her brother getting all this extra attention. We would call it a case of hysterical blindness. It can be cured quite easily.'

'It can? But how?'

The doctor smiled.

'I'll prescribe a pair of *hysterical* glasses for your daughter. It's all right, they'll be quite plain lenses, of course. Just let her wear them for a while – she'll soon get tired of them, I'm sure.'

He called Karenza back into the room.

'Well, my dear, I'm going to give you a pair of glasses which will soon make your eyes better. Take this prescription to your nearest optician and he'll quite probably fix you up on the spot.'

The doctor patted her arm.

'I'm sure you'll find your new glasses a most striking asset. Your friends will all be very impressed. You just wait and see.'

He permitted himself a small chuckle at the witticism.

'Now you can run along.'

Karenza got to her feet and began groping her blind way towards the door. Suddenly she paused dramatically.

'Mummy! Daddy! I *nearly* saw something then. Shapes moving about all weird ... like in a grey mist or something ...'

She still made us go through with taking her to the opticians and buying a perfectly useless pair of plain glasses. She wore these triumphantly for the next few days until, to her own satisfaction, she had completely obliterated the annoying precedent taken in attention by her unfortunate brother, who really did have to wear glasses permanently. Then, one day –

186

the glasses simply weren't there any more.

Karenza ... had embarked on her latest and greatest role, the blind girl who had experienced the Miracle Cure.